On the Track by Henry Lawson

Henry Archibald Hertzberg Lawson was born on the 17th June 1867 in a town on the Grenfell goldfields of New South Wales, Australia.

As a youth an ear infection had left him partially deaf and by fourteen he had lost his hearing completely.

He immersed himself in books to make up for the difficulties of a classroom education but later failed to gain entry to a University.

His first published poem was 'A Song of the Republic' in The Bulletin on 1st October 1887. This was quickly followed by other poems with one recognising him as "a youth whose poetic genius here speaks eloquently for itself."

In 1892, The Bulletin engaged him for an inland trip where he could write articles about the harsh realities of life in drought-stricken New South Wales. This resulted in his contributions to the Bulletin Debate and became the experience for a number of his stories in subsequent years. For Lawson this was an eye-opening period. His grim view of the outback was far removed from the romantic idyll of contemporary poetry and literature.

In 1896, Lawson married Bertha Bredt, Jr. but the marriage ended in June 1903. They had two children.

Despite this Lawson was finding his way in the literary world and achieving recognition. His most successful prose collection 'While the Billy Boils', was published in 1896. In it he virtually reinvented Australian realism.

His writing style of short, sharp sentences with honed and sparse descriptions created a personal writing style that defined Australians: dryly laconic, passionately egalitarian and deeply humane.

Sadly, for Lawson despite his growing recognition and fame he became withdrawn and unable to take part in the usual routines of life. His struggles with alcohol and mental health issues continued to drain him. His once prolific literary output began to decline. At times he was destitute mainly due, despite good sales and an enthusiastic audience, to ruinous publishing deals he had entered into.

Henry Archibald Hertzberg Lawson died, of cerebral hemorrhage, in Abbotsford, Sydney on 2nd September 1922.

Index of Contents

The Songs They used to Sing

On the diggings up to twenty odd years ago—and as far back as I can remember—on Lambing Flat, the Pipe Clays, Gulgong, Home Rule, and so through the roaring list; in bark huts, tents, public-houses, sly grog shanties, and—well, the most glorious voice of all belonged to a bad girl. We were only children and didn't know why she was bad, but we weren't allowed to play near or go near the hut she lived in, and we were trained to believe firmly that something awful would happen to us if we stayed to answer a word, and didn't run away as fast as our legs could carry us, if she attempted to speak to us. We had before us the dread example of one urchin, who got an awful hiding and went on bread and water for twenty-four hours for allowing her to kiss him and give him lollies. She didn't look bad—she looked to us like a grand and beautiful lady-girl—but we got instilled into us the idea that she was an awful bad woman, something more terrible even than a drunken man, and one whose presence was to be feared and fled from. There were two other girls in the hut with her, also a pretty little girl, who called her "Auntie", and with whom we were not allowed to play—for they were all bad; which puzzled us as much as child-minds can be puzzled. We couldn't make out how everybody in one house could be bad. We used to wonder why these bad people weren't hunted away or put in gaol if they were so bad. And another thing puzzled us. Slipping out after dark, when the bad girls happened to be singing in their house, we'd sometimes run against men hanging round the hut by ones and twos and threes, listening. They seemed mysterious. They were mostly good men, and we concluded they were listening and watching the bad women's house to see that they didn't kill anyone, or steal and run away with any bad little boys—ourselves, for instance—who ran out after dark; which, as we were informed, those bad people were always on the lookout for a chance to do.

We were told in after years that old Peter McKenzie (a respectable, married, hard-working digger) would sometimes steal up opposite the bad door in the dark, and throw in money done up in a piece of paper, and listen round until the bad girl had sung the "Bonnie Hills of Scotland" two or three times. Then he'd go and get drunk, and stay drunk two or three days at a time. And his wife caught him throwing the money in one night, and there was a terrible row, and she left him; and people always said it was all a mistake. But we couldn't see the mistake then.

But I can hear that girl's voice through the night, twenty years ago:

Oh! the bloomin' heath, and the pale blue bell,
In my bonnet then I wore;
And memory knows no brighter theme
Than those happy days of yore.
Scotland! Land of chief and song!
Oh, what charms to thee belong!

And I am old enough to understand why poor Peter McKenzie—who was married to a Saxon, and a Tartar—went and got drunk when the bad girl sang "The Bonnie Hills of Scotland."

His anxious eye might look in vain
For some loved form it knew!

And yet another thing puzzled us greatly at the time. Next door to the bad girl's house there lived a very respectable family—a family of good girls with whom we were allowed to play, and from whom we got lollies (those hard old red-and-white "fish lollies" that grocers sent home with parcels of groceries and receipted bills). Now one washing day, they being as glad to get rid of us at home as we were to get out, we went over to the good house and found no one at home except the grown-up daughter, who used to sing for us, and read "Robinson Crusoe" of nights, "out loud", and give us more lollies than any of the rest—and with whom we were passionately in love, notwithstanding the fact that she was engaged to a "grown-up man"—(we reckoned he'd be dead and out of the way by the time we were old enough to marry her). She was washing. She had carried the stool and tub over against the stick fence which separated her house from the bad house; and, to our astonishment and dismay, the bad girl had brought HER tub over against her side of the fence. They stood and worked with their shoulders to the fence between them, and heads bent down close to it. The bad girl would sing a few words, and the good girl after her, over and over again. They sang very low, we thought. Presently the good grown-up girl turned her head and caught sight of us. She jumped, and her face went flaming red; she laid hold of the stool and carried it, tub and all, away from that fence in a hurry. And the bad grown-up girl took her tub back to her house. The good grown-up girl made us promise never to tell what we saw—that she'd been talking to a bad girl—else she would never, never marry us.

She told me, in after years, when she'd grown up to be a grandmother, that the bad girl was surreptitiously teaching her to sing "Madeline" that day.

I remember a dreadful story of a digger who went and shot himself one night after hearing that bad girl sing. We thought then what a frightfully bad woman she must be. The incident terrified us; and thereafter we kept carefully and fearfully out of reach of her voice, lest we should go and do what the digger did.

I have a dreamy recollection of a circus on Gulgong in the roaring days, more than twenty years ago, and a woman (to my child-fancy a being from another world) standing in the middle of the ring, singing:

Out in the cold world—out in the street—
Asking a penny from each one I meet;
Cheerless I wander about all the day,
Wearing my young life in sorrow away!

That last line haunted me for many years. I remember being frightened by women sobbing (and one or two great grown-up diggers also) that night in that circus.

"Father, Dear Father, Come Home with Me Now", was a sacred song then, not a peg for vulgar parodies and more vulgar "business" for fourth-rate clowns and corner-men. Then there was "The Prairie Flower". "Out on the Prairie, in an Early Day"—I can hear the digger's wife yet: she was the prettiest girl on the field. They married on the sly and crept into camp after dark; but the diggers got wind of it and rolled up with gold-dishes, shovels, &c., &c., and gave them a real good tinkettling in the old-fashioned style, and a nugget or two to start housekeeping on. She had a very sweet voice.

Fair as a lily, joyous and free,
Light of the prairie home was she.

She's a "granny" now, no doubt—or dead.

And I remember a poor, brutally ill-used little wife, wearing a black eye mostly, and singing "Love Amongst the Roses" at her work. And they sang the "Blue Tail Fly", and all the first and best coon songs—in the days when old John Brown sank a duffer on the hill.

The great bark kitchen of Granny Mathews' "Redclay Inn". A fresh back-log thrown behind the fire, which lights the room fitfully. Company settled down to pipes, subdued yarning, and reverie.

Flash Jack—red sash, cabbage-tree hat on back of head with nothing in it, glossy black curls bunched up in front of brim. Flash Jack volunteers, without invitation, preparation, or warning, and through his nose:

Hoh!—
There was a wild kerlonial youth,
John Dowlin was his name!
He bountied on his parients,
Who lived in Castlemaine!

and so on to—

He took a pistol from his breast
And waved that lit—tle toy—

"Little toy" with an enthusiastic flourish and great unction on Flash Jack's part—

"I'll fight, but I won't surrender!" said
The wild Kerlonial Boy.

Even this fails to rouse the company's enthusiasm. "Give us a song, Abe! Give us the 'Lowlands'!" Abe Mathews, bearded and grizzled, is lying on the broad of his back on a bench, with his hands clasped under his head—his favourite position for smoking, reverie, yarning, or singing. He had a strong, deep voice, which used to thrill me through and through, from hair to toenails, as a child.

They bother Abe till he takes his pipe out of his mouth and puts it behind his head on the end of the stool:

The ship was built in Glasgow;
'Twas the "Golden Vanitee"— Lines have dropped out of my memory during the thirty years gone between—

And she ploughed in the Low Lands, Low!

The public-house people and more diggers drop into the kitchen, as all do within hearing, when Abe sings.

"Now then, boys:

And she ploughed in the Low Lands, Low!

"Now, all together!

The Low Lands! The Low Lands!
And she ploughed in the Low Lands, Low!"

Toe and heel and flat of foot begin to stamp the clay floor, and horny hands to slap patched knees in accompaniment.

"Oh! save me, lads!" he cried,
"I'm drifting with the current,
And I'm drifting with the tide!
And I'm sinking in the Low Lands, Low!
The Low Lands! The Low Lands!"—

The old bark kitchen is a-going now. Heels drumming on gin-cases under stools; hands, knuckles, pipe-bowls, and pannikins keeping time on the table.

And we sewed him in his hammock,
And we slipped him o'er the side,
And we sunk him in the Low Lands, Low!
The Low Lands! The Low Lands!
And we sunk him in the Low Lands, Low!

Old Boozer Smith—a dirty gin-sodden bundle of rags on the floor in the corner with its head on a candle box, and covered by a horse rug—old Boozer Smith is supposed to have been dead to the universe for hours past, but the chorus must have disturbed his torpor; for, with a suddenness and unexpectedness that makes the next man jump, there comes a bellow from under the horse rug:

Wot though!—I wear!—a rag!—ged coat!
I'll wear it like a man!

and ceases as suddenly as it commenced. He struggles to bring his ruined head and bloated face above the surface, glares round; then, no one questioning his manhood, he sinks back and dies to creation; and subsequent proceedings are only interrupted by a snore, as far as he is concerned.

Little Jimmy Nowlett, the bullock-driver, is inspired. "Go on, Jimmy! Give us a song!"

In the days when we were hard up
For want of wood and wire— Jimmy always blunders; it should have been "food and fire"—

We used to tie our boots up
With lit—tle bits—er wire;

and—

I'm sitting in my lit—tle room,
It measures six by six;
The work-house wall is opposite,
I've counted all the bricks!

"Give us a chorus, Jimmy!"

Jimmy does, giving his head a short, jerky nod for nearly every word, and describing a circle round his crown—as if he were stirring a pint of hot tea—with his forefinger, at the end of every line:

Hall!—Round!—Me—Hat!
I wore a weepin' willer!

Jimmy is a Cockney.

"Now then, boys!"

Hall—round—me hat!

How many old diggers remember it?

And:

A butcher, and a baker, and a quiet-looking quaker,
All a-courting pretty Jessie at the Railway Bar.

I used to wonder as a child what the "railway bar" meant.

And:

I would, I would, I would in vain
That I were single once again!
But ah, alas, that will not be
Till apples grow on the willow tree.

A drunken gambler's young wife used to sing that song—to herself.

A stir at the kitchen door, and a cry of "Pinter," and old Poynton, Ballarat digger, appears and is shoved in; he has several drinks aboard, and they proceed to "git Pinter on the singin' lay," and at last talk him round. He has a good voice, but no "theory", and blunders worse than Jimmy Nowlett with the words. He starts with a howl—

Hoh!
Way down in Covent Gar-ar-r-dings
A-strolling I did go,
To see the sweetest flow-ow-wers
That e'er in gardings grow.

He saw the rose and lily—the red and white and blue—and he saw the sweetest flow-ow-ers that e'er in gardings grew; for he saw two lovely maidens (Pinter calls 'em "virgings") underneath (he must have meant on top of) "a garding chair", sings Pinter.

And one was lovely Jessie,
With the jet black eyes and hair,

roars Pinter,

And the other was a vir-ir-ging,
I solemn-lye declare!

"Maiden, Pinter!" interjects Mr. Nowlett.

"Well, it's all the same," retorts Pinter. "A maiden IS a virging, Jimmy. If you're singing, Jimmy, and not me, I'll leave off!" Chorus of "Order! Shut up, Jimmy!"

I quicklye step-ped up to her,
And unto her did sa-a-y:
Do you belong to any young man,
Hoh, tell me that, I pra-a-y?

Her answer, according to Pinter, was surprisingly prompt and unconventional; also full and concise:

No; I belong to no young man—
I solemnlye declare!
I mean to live a virging
And still my laurels wear!

Jimmy Nowlett attempts to move an amendment in favour of "maiden", but is promptly suppressed. It seems that Pinter's suit has a happy termination, for he is supposed to sing in the character of a "Sailor Bold", and as he turns to pursue his stroll in "Covent Gar-ar-dings":

"Oh, no! Oh, no! Oh, no!" she cried,

"I love a Sailor Bold!"

"Hong-kore, Pinter! Give us the 'Golden Glove', Pinter!"

Thus warmed up, Pinter starts with an explanatory "spoken" to the effect that the song he is about to sing illustrates some of the little ways of woman, and how, no matter what you say or do, she is bound to have her own way in the end; also how, in one instance, she set about getting it.

Hoh!

Now, it's of a young squoire near Timworth did dwell,
Who courted a nobleman's daughter so well—

The song has little or nothing to do with the "squire", except so far as "all friends and relations had given consent," and—

The troo-soo was ordered—appointed the day,
And a farmer were appointed for to give her away—

which last seemed a most unusual proceeding, considering the wedding was a toney affair; but perhaps there were personal interests—the nobleman might have been hard up, and the farmer backing him. But there was an extraordinary scene in the church, and things got mixed.

For as soon as this maiding this farmer espied:
"Hoh, my heart! Hoh, my heart!
Hoh, my heart!" then she cried.

Hysterics? Anyway, instead of being wed—

This maiden took sick and she went to her bed.

(N.B.—Pinter sticks to 'virging'.)

Whereupon friends and relations and guests left the house in a body (a strange but perhaps a wise proceeding, after all—maybe they smelt a rat) and left her to recover alone, which she did promptly. And then:

Shirt, breeches, and waistcoat this maiding put on,
And a-hunting she went with her dog and her gun;
She hunted all round where this farmier did dwell,
Because in her own heart she love-ed him well.

The cat's out of the bag now:

And often she fired, but no game she killed—

which was not surprising—

Till at last the young farmier came into the field—

No wonder. She put it to him straight:

"Oh, why are you not at the wedding?" she cried,
"For to wait on the squoire, and to give him his bride."

He was as prompt and as delightfully unconventional in his reply as the young lady in Covent Gardings:

"Oh, no! and oh, no! For the truth I must sa-a-y,
I love her too well for to give her a-w-a-a-y!"

which was satisfactory to the disguised "virging".

".... and I'd take sword in hand,
And by honour I'd win her if she would command."

Which was still more satisfactory.

Now this virging, being— (Jimmy Nowlett: "Maiden, Pinter—" Jim is thrown on a stool and sat on by several diggers.)

Now this maiding, being please-ed to see him so bold,
She gave him her glove that was flowered with gold,

and explained that she found it in his field while hunting around with her dog and her gun. It is understood that he promised to look up the owner. Then she went home and put an advertisement in the local 'Herald'; and that ad. must have caused considerable sensation. She stated that she had lost her golden glove, and

The young man that finds it and brings it to me,
Hoh! that very young man my husband shall be!

She had a saving clause in case the young farmer mislaid the glove before he saw the ad., and an OLD bloke got holt of it and fetched it along. But everything went all right. The young farmer turned up with the glove. He was a very respectable young farmer, and expressed his gratitude to her for having "honour-ed him with her love." They were married, and the song ends with a picture of the young farmeress milking the cow, and the young farmer going whistling to plough. The fact that they lived and grafted on the selection proves that I hit the right nail on the head when I guessed, in the first place, that the old nobleman was "stony".

In after years,

... she told him of the fun,
How she hunted him up with her dog and her gun.

But whether he was pleased or otherwise to hear it, after years of matrimonial experiences, the old song doesn't say, for it ends there.

Flash Jack is more successful with "Saint Patrick's Day".

I come to the river, I jumped it quite clever!
Me wife tumbled in, and I lost her for ever,
St. Patrick's own day in the mornin'!

This is greatly appreciated by Jimmy Nowlett, who is suspected, especially by his wife, of being more cheerful when on the roads than when at home.

"Sam Holt" was a great favourite with Jimmy Nowlett in after years.

Oh, do you remember Black Alice, Sam Holt?
Black Alice so dirty and dark—
Who'd a nose on her face—I forget how it goes—
And teeth like a Moreton Bay shark.

Sam Holt must have been very hard up for tucker as well as beauty then, for

Do you remember the 'possums and grubs
She baked for you down by the creek?

Sam Holt was, apparently, a hardened flash Jack.

You were not quite the cleanly potato, Sam Holt.

Reference is made to his "manner of holding a flush", and he is asked to remember several things which he, no doubt, would rather forget, including

... the hiding you got from the boys.

The song is decidedly personal.

But Sam Holt makes a pile and goes home, leaving many a better and worse man to pad the hoof Out Back. And—Jim Nowlett sang this with so much feeling as to make it appear a personal affair between him and the absent Holt—

And, don't you remember the fiver, Sam Holt,
You borrowed so careless and free?
I reckon I'll whistle a good many tunes

(with increasing feeling)

Ere you think of that fiver and me.

For the chances will be that Sam Holt's old mate

Will be humping his drum on the Hughenden Road

To the end of the chapter of fate.

An echo from "The Old Bark Hut", sung in the opposition camp across the gully:

You may leave the door ajar, but if you keep it shut,
There's no need of suffocation in the Ould Barrk Hut.

The tucker's in the gin-case, but you'd better keep it shut—
For the flies will canther round it in the Ould Bark Hut.

However:

What's out of sight is out of mind, in the Ould Bark Hut.

We washed our greasy moleskins
On the banks of the Condamine.—

Somebody tackling the "Old Bullock Dray"; it must be over fifty verses now. I saw a bushman at a country dance start to sing that song; he'd get up to ten or fifteen verses, break down, and start afresh. At last he sat down on his heel to it, in the centre of the clear floor, resting his wrist on his knee, and keeping time with an index finger. It was very funny, but the thing was taken seriously all through.

Irreverent echo from the old Lambing Flat trouble, from camp across the gully:

Rule Britannia! Britannia rules the waves!
No more Chinamen will enter Noo South Wales!

and

Yankee Doodle came to town
On a little pony—
Stick a feather in his cap,
And call him Maccaroni!

All the camps seem to be singing to-night:

Ring the bell, watchman!
Ring! Ring! Ring!
Ring, for the good news
Is now on the wing!

Good lines, the introduction:

High on the belfry the old sexton stands,
Grasping the rope with his thin bony hands!...
Bon-fires are blazing throughout the land...
Glorious and blessed tidings! Ring! Ring the bell!

Granny Mathews fails to coax her niece into the kitchen, but persuades her to sing inside. She is the girl who learnt 'sub rosa' from the bad girl who sang "Madeline". Such as have them on instinctively take their hats off. Diggers, &c., strolling past, halt at the first notes of the girl's voice, and stand like statues in the moonlight:

Shall we gather at the river,
Where bright angel feet have trod?
The beautiful—the beautiful river
That flows by the throne of God!—

Diggers wanted to send that girl "Home", but Granny Mathews had the old-fashioned horror of any of her children becoming "public"—

Gather with the saints at the river,
That flows by the throne of God!

But it grows late, or rather, early. The "Eyetalians" go by in the frosty moonlight, from their last shift in the claim (for it is Saturday night), singing a litany.

"Get up on one end, Abe!—stand up all!" Hands are clasped across the kitchen table. Redclay, one of the last of the alluvial fields, has petered out, and the Roaring Days are dying.... The grand old song that is known all over the world; yet how many in ten thousand know more than one verse and the chorus? Let Peter McKenzie lead:

Should auld acquaintance be forgot,
And never brought to min'?

And hearts echo from far back in the past and across wide, wide seas:

Should auld acquaintance be forgot,
And days o' lang syne?

Now boys! all together!

For auld lang syne, my dear,
For auld lang syne,
We'll tak' a cup o' kindness yet,
For auld lang syne.

We twa hae run about the braes,
And pu'd the gowans fine;
But we've wandered mony a weary foot,
Sin' auld lang syne.

The world was wide then.

We twa hae paidl't i' the burn,
Frae mornin' sun till dine:

the log fire seems to grow watery, for in wide, lonely Australia—
But seas between us braid hae roar'd,
Sin' auld lang syne.

The kitchen grows dimmer, and the forms of the digger-singers seemed suddenly vague and unsubstantial, fading back rapidly through a misty veil. But the words ring strong and defiant through hard years:

And here's a hand, my trusty frien',
And gie's a grup o' thine;
And we'll tak' a cup o' kindness yet,
For auld lang syne.

And the nettles have been growing for over twenty years on the spot where Granny Mathews' big bark kitchen stood.

A Vision of Sandy Blight

I'd been humping my back, and crouching and groaning for an hour or so in the darkest corner of the travellers' hut, tortured by the demon of sandy blight. It was too hot to travel, and there was no one there except ourselves and Mitchell's cattle pup. We were waiting till after sundown, for I couldn't have travelled in the daylight, anyway. Mitchell had tied a wet towel round my eyes, and led me for the last mile or two by another towel—one end fastened to his belt behind, and the other in my hand as I walked in his tracks. And oh! but this was a relief! It was out of the dust and glare, and the flies didn't come into the dark hut, and I could hump and stick my knees in my eyes and groan in comfort. I didn't want a thousand a year, or anything; I only wanted relief for my eyes—that was all I prayed for in this world. When the sun got down a bit, Mitchell started poking round, and presently he found amongst the rubbish a dirty-looking medicine bottle, corked tight; when he rubbed the dirt off a piece of notepaper that was pasted on, he saw "eye-water" written on it. He drew the cork with his teeth, smelt the water, stuck his little finger in, turned the bottle upside down, tasted the top of his finger, and reckoned the stuff was all right.

"Here! Wake up, Joe!" he shouted. "Here's a bottle of tears."

"A bottler wot?" I groaned.

"Eye-water," said Mitchell.

"Are you sure it's all right?" I didn't want to be poisoned or have my eyes burnt out by mistake; perhaps some burning acid had got into that bottle, or the label had been put on, or left on, in mistake or carelessness.

"I dunno," said Mitchell, "but there's no harm in tryin'."

I chanced it. I lay down on my back in a bunk, and Mitchell dragged my lids up and spilt half a bottle of eye-water over my eye-balls.

The relief was almost instantaneous. I never experienced such a quick cure in my life. I carried the bottle in my swag for a long time afterwards, with an idea of getting it analysed, but left it behind at last in a camp.

Mitchell scratched his head thoughtfully, and watched me for a while.

"I think I'll wait a bit longer," he said at last, "and if it doesn't blind you I'll put some in my eyes. I'm getting a touch of blight myself now. That's the fault of travelling with a mate who's always catching something that's no good to him."

As it grew dark outside we talked of sandy-blight and fly-bite, and sand-flies up north, and ordinary flies, and branched off to Barcoo rot, and struck the track again at bees and bee stings. When we got to bees, Mitchell sat smoking for a while and looking dreamily backwards along tracks and branch tracks, and round corners and circles he had travelled, right back to the short, narrow, innocent bit of track that ends in a vague, misty point—like the end of a long, straight, cleared road in the moonlight—as far back as we can remember.

"I had about fourteen hives," said Mitchell—"we used to call them 'swarms', no matter whether they were flying or in the box—when I left home first time. I kept them behind the shed, in the shade, on tables of galvanised iron cases turned down on stakes; but I had to make legs later on, and stand them in pans of water, on account of the ants. When the bees swarmed—and some hives sent out the Lord knows how many swarms in a year, it seemed to me—we'd tin-kettle 'em, and throw water on 'em, to make 'em believe the biggest thunderstorm was coming to drown the oldest inhabitant; and, if they didn't get the start of us and rise, they'd settle on a branch—generally on one of the scraggy fruit trees. It was rough on the bees—come to think of it; their instinct told them it was going to be fine, and the noise and water told them it was raining. They must have thought that nature was mad, drunk, or gone ratty, or the end of the world had come. We'd rig up a table, with a box upside down, under the branch, cover our face with a piece of mosquito net, have rags burning round, and then give the branch a sudden jerk, turn the box down, and run. If we got most of the bees in, the rest that were hanging to the bough or flying round would follow, and then we reckoned we'd shook the queen in. If the bees in the box came out and joined the others, we'd reckon we hadn't shook the queen in, and go for them again. When a hive was full of honey we'd turn the box upside down, turn the empty box mouth down on top of it, and drum and hammer on the lower box with a stick till all the bees went up into the top box. I suppose it made their heads ache, and they went up on that account.

"I suppose things are done differently on proper bee-farms. I've heard that a bee-farmer will part a hanging swarm with his fingers, take out the queen bee and arrange matters with her; but our ways suited us, and there was a lot of expectation and running and excitement in it, especially when a swarm took us by surprise. The yell of 'Bees swarmin'!' was as good to us as the yell of 'Fight!' is now, or 'Bolt!' in town, or 'Fire' or 'Man overboard!' at sea.

"There was tons of honey. The bees used to go to the vineyards at wine-making and get honey from the heaps of crushed grape-skins thrown out in the sun, and get so drunk sometimes that they wobbled in their bee-lines home. They'd fill all the boxes, and then build in between and under the bark, and board, and tin covers. They never seemed to get the idea out of their heads that this wasn't an evergreen country, and it wasn't going to snow all winter. My younger brother Joe used to put pieces of meat on the tables near the boxes, and in front of the holes where the bees went in and out, for the dogs to grab at. But one old dog, 'Black Bill', was a match for him; if it was worth Bill's while, he'd camp there, and keep Joe and the other dogs from touching the meat—once it was put down—till the bees turned in for the night. And Joe would get the other kids round there, and when they weren't looking or thinking, he'd brush the bees with a stick and run. I'd lam him when I caught him at it. He was an awful young devil, was Joe, and he grew up steady, and respectable, and respected—and I went to the bad. I never trust a good boy now.... Ah, well!

"I remember the first swarm we got. We'd been talking of getting a few swarms for a long time. That was what was the matter with us English and Irish and English-Irish Australian farmers: we used to talk so much about doing things while the Germans and Scotch did them. And we even talked in a lazy, easy-going sort of way.

"Well, one blazing hot day I saw father coming along the road, home to dinner (we had it in the middle of the day), with his axe over his shoulder. I noticed the axe particularly because father was bringing it home to grind, and Joe and I had to turn the stone; but, when I noticed Joe dragging along home in the dust about fifty yards behind father, I felt easier in my mind. Suddenly father dropped the axe and started to run back along the road towards Joe, who, as soon as he saw father coming, shied for the fence and got through. He thought he was going to catch it for something he'd done—or hadn't done. Joe used to do so many things and leave so many things not done that he could never be sure of father. Besides, father had a way of starting to hammer us unexpectedly—when the idea struck him. But father pulled himself up in about thirty yards and started to grab up handfuls of dust and sand and throw them into the air. My idea, in the first flash, was to get hold of the axe, for I thought it was sun-stroke, and father might take it into his head to start chopping up the family before I could persuade him to put it (his head, I mean) in a bucket of water. But Joe came running like mad, yelling:

"'Swarmer—bees! Swawmmer—bee—ee—es! Bring—a—tin—dish—and—a—dippera—wa-a-ter!'

"I ran with a bucket of water and an old frying-pan, and pretty soon the rest of the family were on the spot, throwing dust and water, and banging everything, tin or iron, they could get hold of. The only bullock bell in the district (if it was in the district) was on the old poley cow, and she'd been lost for a fortnight. Mother brought up the rear—but soon worked to the front—with a baking-dish and a big spoon. The old lady—she wasn't old then—had a deep-rooted prejudice that she could do everything better than anybody else, and that the selection and all on it would go to the dogs if she wasn't there to look after it. There was no jolting that idea out of her. She not only believed that she could do anything better than anybody, and hers was the only right or possible way, and that we'd do everything upside down if she wasn't there to do it or show us how—but she'd try to do things herself or insist on making us do them her way, and that led to messes and rows. She was excited now, and took command at once. She wasn't tongue-tied, and had no impediment in her speech.

"'Don't throw up dust!—Stop throwing up dust!—Do you want to smother 'em?—Don't throw up so much water!—Only throw up a pannikin at a time!—D'yer want to drown 'em? Bang! Keep on banging, Joe!—Look at that child! Run, someone!—run! you, Jack!—D'yer want the child to be stung to death?—Take her inside!... Dy' hear me?... Stop throwing up dust, Tom! (To father.) You're scaring 'em away! Can't you see they want to settle?' [Father was getting mad and yelping: 'For Godsake shettup and go inside.'] 'Throw up water, Jack! Throw up—Tom! Take that bucket from him and don't make such a fool of yourself before the children! Throw up water! Throw—keep on banging, children! Keep on banging!'

[Mother put her faith in banging.] 'There!—they're off! You've lost 'em! I knew you would! I told yer—keep on bang—!'

"A bee struck her in the eye, and she grabbed at it!

"Mother went home—and inside.

"Father was good at bees—could manage them like sheep when he got to know their ideas. When the swarm settled, he sent us for the old washing stool, boxes, bags, and so on; and the whole time he was fixing the bees I noticed that whenever his back was turned to us his shoulders would jerk up as if he was cold, and he seemed to shudder from inside, and now and then I'd hear a grunting sort of whimper like a boy that was just starting to blubber. But father wasn't weeping, and bees weren't stinging him; it was the bee that stung mother that was tickling father. When he went into the house, mother's other eye had bunged for sympathy. Father was always gentle and kind in sickness, and he bathed mother's eyes and rubbed mud on, but every now and then he'd catch inside, and jerk and shudder, and grunt and cough. Mother got wild, but presently the humour of it struck her, and she had to laugh, and a rum laugh it was, with both eyes bunged up. Then she got hysterical, and started to cry, and father put his arm round her shoulder and ordered us out of the house.

"They were very fond of each other, the old people were, under it all—right up to the end.... Ah, well!"

Mitchell pulled the swags out of a bunk, and started to fasten the nose-bags on.

Andy Page's Rival

Tall and freckled and sandy,
Face of a country lout;
That was the picture of Andy—
Middleton's rouseabout.
On Middleton's wide dominions
Plied the stock-whip and shears;
Hadn't any opinions—

And he hadn't any "ideers"—at least, he said so himself—except as regarded anything that looked to him like what he called "funny business", under which heading he catalogued tyranny, treachery, interference with the liberty of the subject by the subject, "blanky" lies, or swindles—all things, in short, that seemed to his slow understanding dishonest, mean or paltry; most especially, and above all, treachery to a mate. THAT he could never forget. Andy was uncomfortably "straight". His mind worked slowly and his decisions were, as a rule, right and just; and when he once came to a conclusion concerning any man or matter, or decided upon a course of action, nothing short of an earthquake or a Nevertire cyclone could move him back an inch—unless a conviction were severely shaken, and then he would require as much time to "back" to his starting point as he did to come to the decision.

Andy had come to a conclusion with regard to a selector's daughter—name, Lizzie Porter—who lived (and slaved) on her father's selection, near the township corner of the run on which Andy was a general "hand". He had been in the habit for several years of calling casually at the selector's house, as he rode to and fro between the station and the town, to get a drink of water and exchange the time of day with old Porter and his "missus". The conversation concerned the drought, and the likelihood or otherwise of their ever going to get a little rain; or about Porter's cattle, with an occasional enquiry concerning, or reference to, a stray cow belonging to the selection, but preferring the run; a little, plump, saucy, white cow, by-the-way, practically pure white, but referred to by Andy—who had eyes like a blackfellow—as "old Speckledy". No one else could detect a spot or speckle on her at a casual glance. Then after a long bovine silence, which would have been painfully embarrassing in any other society, and a tilting of his cabbage-tree hat forward, which came of tickling and scratching the sun-blotched nape of his neck with his little finger, Andy would slowly say: "Ah, well. I must be gettin'. So-long, Mr. Porter. So-long, Mrs. Porter." And, if SHE were in evidence—as she generally was on such occasions—"So-long, Lizzie." And they'd shout: "So-long, Andy," as he galloped off from the jump. Strange that those shy, quiet, gentle-voiced bushmen seem the hardest and most reckless riders.

But of late his horse had been seen hanging up outside Porter's for an hour or so after sunset. He smoked, talked over the results of the last drought (if it happened to rain), and the possibilities of the next one, and played cards with old Porter; who took to winking, automatically, at his "old woman", and nudging, and jerking his thumb in the direction of Lizzie when her back was turned, and Andy was scratching the nape of his neck and staring at the cards.

Lizzie told a lady friend of mine, years afterwards, how Andy popped the question; told it in her quiet way—you know Lizzie's quiet way (something of the old, privileged house-cat about her); never a sign in expression or tone to show whether she herself saw or appreciated the humour of anything she was telling, no matter how comical it might be. She had witnessed two tragedies, and had found a dead man in the bush, and related the incidents as though they were common-place.

It happened one day—after Andy had been coming two or three times a week for about a year—that she found herself sitting with him on a log of the woodheap, in the cool of the evening, enjoying the sunset breeze. Andy's arm had got round her—just as it might have gone round a post he happened to be leaning against. They hadn't been talking about anything in particular. Andy said he wouldn't be surprised if they had a thunderstorm before mornin'—it had been so smotherin' hot all day.

Lizzie said, "Very likely."

Andy smoked a good while, then he said: "Ah, well! It's a weary world."

Lizzie didn't say anything.

By-and-bye Andy said: "Ah, well; it's a lonely world, Lizzie."

"Do you feel lonely, Andy?" asked Lizzie, after a while.

"Yes, Lizzie; I do."

Lizzie let herself settle, a little, against him, without either seeming to notice it, and after another while she said, softly: "So do I, Andy."

Andy knocked the ashes from his pipe very slowly and deliberately, and put it away; then he seemed to brighten suddenly, and said briskly: "Well, Lizzie! Are you satisfied!"

"Yes, Andy; I'm satisfied."

"Quite sure, now?"

"Yes; I'm quite sure, Andy. I'm perfectly satisfied."

"Well, then, Lizzie—it's settled!"

But to-day—a couple of months after the proposal described above—Andy had trouble on his mind, and the trouble was connected with Lizzie Porter. He was putting up a two-rail fence along the old log-paddock on the frontage, and working like a man in trouble, trying to work it off his mind; and evidently not succeeding—for the last two panels were out of line. He was ramming a post—Andy rammed honestly, from the bottom of the hole, not the last few shovelfuls below the surface, as some do. He was ramming the last layer of clay when a cloud of white dust came along the road, paused, and drifted or poured off into the scrub, leaving long Dave Bentley, the horse-breaker, on his last victim.

"'Ello, Andy! Graftin'?"

"I want to speak to you, Dave," said Andy, in a strange voice.

"All—all right!" said Dave, rather puzzled. He got down, wondering what was up, and hung his horse to the last post but one.

Dave was Andy's opposite in one respect: he jumped to conclusions, as women do; but, unlike women, he was mostly wrong. He was an old chum and mate of Andy's who had always liked, admired, and trusted him. But now, to his helpless surprise, Andy went on scraping the earth from the surface with his long-handled shovel, and heaping it conscientiously round the butt of the post, his face like a block of wood, and his lips set grimly. Dave broke out first (with bush oaths):

"What's the matter with you? Spit it out! What have I been doin' to you? What's yer got yer rag out about, anyway?"

Andy faced him suddenly, with hatred for "funny business" flashing in his eyes.

"What did you say to my sister Mary about Lizzie Porter?"

Dave started; then he whistled long and low. "Spit it all out, Andy!" he advised.

"You said she was travellin' with a feller!"

"Well, what's the harm in that? Everybody knows that—"

"If any crawler says a word about Lizzie Porter—look here, me and you's got to fight, Dave Bentley!" Then, with still greater vehemence, as though he had a share in the garment: "Take off that coat!"

"Not if I know it!" said Dave, with the sudden quietness that comes to brave but headstrong and impulsive men at a critical moment: "Me and you ain't goin' to fight, Andy; and" (with sudden energy) "if you try it on I'll knock you into jim-rags!"

Then, stepping close to Andy and taking him by the arm: "Andy, this thing will have to be fixed up. Come here; I want to talk to you." And he led him some paces aside, inside the boundary line, which seemed a ludicrously unnecessary precaution, seeing that there was no one within sight or hearing save Dave's horse.

"Now, look here, Andy; let's have it over. What's the matter with you and Lizzie Porter?"

"I'M travellin' with her, that's all; and we're going to get married in two years!"

Dave gave vent to another long, low whistle. He seemed to think and make up his mind.

"Now, look here, Andy: we're old mates, ain't we?"

"Yes; I know that."

"And do you think I'd tell you a blanky lie, or crawl behind your back? Do you? Spit it out!"

"N—no, I don't!"

"I've always stuck up for you, Andy, and—why, I've fought for you behind your back!"

"I know that, Dave."

"There's my hand on it!"

Andy took his friend's hand mechanically, but gripped it hard.

"Now, Andy, I'll tell you straight: It's Gorstruth about Lizzie Porter!"

They stood as they were for a full minute, hands clasped; Andy with his jaw dropped and staring in a dazed sort of way at Dave. He raised his disengaged hand helplessly to his thatch, gulped suspiciously, and asked in a broken voice:

"How—how do you know it, Dave?"

"Know it? Andy, I SEEN 'EM MESELF!"

"You did, Dave?" in a tone that suggested sorrow more than anger at Dave's part in the seeing of them.

"Gorstruth, Andy!"

"Tell me, Dave, who was the feller? That's all I want to know."

"I can't tell you that. I only seen them when I was canterin' past in the dusk."

"Then how'd you know it was a man at all?"

"It wore trousers, anyway, and was as big as you; so it couldn't have been a girl. I'm pretty safe to swear it was Mick Kelly. I saw his horse hangin' up at Porter's once or twice. But I'll tell you what I'll do: I'll find out for you, Andy. And, what's more, I'll job him for you if I catch him!"

Andy said nothing; his hands clenched and his chest heaved. Dave laid a friendly hand on his shoulder.

"It's red hot, Andy, I know. Anybody else but you and I wouldn't have cared. But don't be a fool; there's any Gorsquantity of girls knockin' round. You just give it to her straight and chuck her, and have done with it. You must be bad off to bother about her. Gorstruth! she ain't much to look at anyway! I've got to ride like blazes to catch the coach. Don't knock off till I come back; I won't be above an hour. I'm goin' to give you some points in case you've got to fight Mick; and I'll have to be there to back you!" And, thus taking the right moment instinctively, he jumped on his horse and galloped on towards the town.

His dust-cloud had scarcely disappeared round a corner of the paddocks when Andy was aware of another one coming towards him. He had a dazed idea that it was Dave coming back, but went on digging another post-hole, mechanically, until a spring-cart rattled up, and stopped opposite him. Then he lifted his head. It was Lizzie herself, driving home from town. She turned towards him with her usual faint smile. Her small features were "washed out" and rather haggard.

"'Ello, Andy!"

But, at the sight of her, all his hatred of "funny business"—intensified, perhaps, by a sense of personal injury—came to a head, and he exploded:

"Look here, Lizzie Porter! I know all about you. You needn't think you're goin' to cotton on with me any more after this! I wouldn't be seen in a paddock with yer! I'm satisfied about you! Get on out of this!"

The girl stared at him for a moment thunderstruck; then she lammed into the old horse with a stick she carried in place of a whip.

She cried, and wondered what she'd done, and trembled so that she could scarcely unharness the horse, and wondered if Andy had got a touch of the sun, and went in and sat down and cried again; and pride came to her aid and she hated Andy; thought of her big brother, away droving, and made a cup of tea. She shed tears over the tea, and went through it all again.

Meanwhile Andy was suffering a reaction. He started to fill the hole before he put the post in; then to ram the post before the rails were in position. Dubbing off the ends of the rails, he was in danger of amputating a toe or a foot with every stroke of the adze. And, at last, trying to squint along the little lumps of clay which he had placed in the centre of the top of each post for several panels back—to assist him to take a line—he found that they swam and doubled, and ran off in watery angles, for his eyes were too moist to see straight and single.

Then he threw down the tools hopelessly, and was standing helplessly undecided whether to go home or go down to the creek and drown himself, when Dave turned up again.

"Seen her?" asked Dave.

"Yes," said Andy.

"Did you chuck her?"

"Look here, Dave; are you sure the feller was Mick Kelly?"

"I never said I was. How was I to know? It was dark. You don't expect I'd 'fox' a feller I see doing a bit of a bear-up to a girl, do you? It might have been you, for all I knowed. I suppose she's been talking you round?"

"No, she ain't," said Andy. "But, look here, Dave; I was properly gone on that girl, I was, and—and I want to be sure I'm right."

The business was getting altogether too psychological for Dave Bentley. "You might as well," he rapped out, "call me a liar at once!"

"'Taint that at all, Dave. I want to get at who the feller is; that's what I want to get at now. Where did you see them, and when?"

"I seen them Anniversary night, along the road, near Ross' farm; and I seen 'em Sunday night afore that—in the trees near the old culvert—near Porter's sliprails; and I seen 'em one night outside Porter's, on a log near the woodheap. They was thick that time, and bearin' up proper, and no mistake. So I can swear to her. Now, are you satisfied about her?"

But Andy was wildly pitchforking his thatch under his hat with all ten fingers and staring at Dave, who began to regard him uneasily; then there came to Andy's eyes an awful glare, which caused Dave to step back hastily.

"Good God, Andy! Are yer goin' ratty?"

"No!" cried Andy, wildly.

"Then what the blazes is the matter with you? You'll have rats if you don't look out!"

"JIMMINY FROTH!—It was ME all the time!"

"What?"

"It was me that was with her all them nights. It was me that you seen. WHY, I POPPED ON THE WOODHEAP!"

Dave was taken too suddenly to whistle this time.

"And you went for her just now?"

"Yes!" yelled Andy.

"Well—you've done it!"

"Yes," said Andy, hopelessly; "I've done it!"

Dave whistled now—a very long, low whistle. "Well, you're a bloomin' goat, Andy, after this. But this thing'll have to be fixed up!" and he cantered away. Poor Andy was too badly knocked to notice the abruptness of Dave's departure, or to see that he turned through the sliprails on to the track that led to Porter's.

Half an hour later Andy appeared at Porter's back door, with an expression on his face as though the funeral was to start in ten minutes. In a tone befitting such an occasion, he wanted to see Lizzie.

Dave had been there with the laudable determination of fixing the business up, and had, of course, succeeded in making it much worse than it was before. But Andy made it all right.

The Iron-Bark Chip

Dave Regan and party—bush-fencers, tank-sinkers, rough carpenters, &c.—were finishing the third and last culvert of their contract on the last section of the new railway line, and had already sent in their vouchers for the completed contract, so that there might be no excuse for extra delay in connection with the cheque.

Now it had been expressly stipulated in the plans and specifications that the timber for certain beams and girders was to be iron-bark and no other, and Government inspectors were authorised to order the removal from the ground of any timber or material they might deem inferior, or not in accordance with the stipulations. The railway contractor's foreman and inspector of sub-contractors was a practical man and a bushman, but he had been a timber-getter himself; his sympathies were bushy, and he was on winking terms with Dave Regan. Besides, extended time was expiring, and the contractors were in a hurry to complete the line. But the Government inspector was a reserved man who poked round on his independent own and appeared in lonely spots at unexpected times—with apparently no definite object in life—like a grey kangaroo bothered by a new wire fence, but unsuspicious of the presence of humans. He wore a grey suit, rode, or mostly led, an ashen-grey horse; the grass was long and grey, so he was seldom spotted until he was well within the horizon and bearing leisurely down on a party of sub-contractors, leading his horse.

Now iron-bark was scarce and distant on those ridges, and another timber, similar in appearance, but much inferior in grain and "standing" quality, was plentiful and close at hand. Dave and party were "about full of" the job and place, and wanted to get their cheque and be gone to another "spec" they had in view. So they came to reckon they'd get the last girder from a handy tree, and have it squared, in place, and carefully and conscientiously tarred before the inspector happened along, if he did. But they didn't. They got it squared, and ready to be lifted into its place; the kindly darkness of tar was ready to cover a fraud that took four strong men with crowbars and levers to shift; and now (such is the regular cussedness of things) as the fraudulent piece of timber lay its last hour on the ground, looking and smelling, to their guilty imaginations like anything but iron-bark, they were aware of the Government inspector drifting down upon them obliquely, with something of the atmosphere of a casual Bill or Jim who had dropped out of his easy-going track to see how they were getting on, and borrow a match. They had more than half hoped that, as he had visited them pretty frequently during the progress of the work, and knew how near it was to completion, he wouldn't bother coming any more. But it's the way with the Government. You might move heaven and earth in vain endeavour to get the "Guvermunt" to flutter an eyelash over something of the most momentous importance to yourself and mates and the district—even to the country; but just when you are leaving authority severely alone, and have strong reasons for not wanting to worry or interrupt it, and not desiring it to worry about you, it will take a fancy into its head to come along and bother.

"It's always the way!" muttered Dave to his mates. "I knew the beggar would turn up!... And the only cronk log we've had, too!" he added, in an injured tone. "If this had 'a' been the only blessed iron-bark in the whole contract, it would have been all right.... Good-day, sir!" (to the inspector). "It's hot?"

The inspector nodded. He was not of an impulsive nature. He got down from his horse and looked at the girder in an abstracted way; and presently there came into his eyes a dreamy, far-away, sad sort of expression, as if there had been a very sad and painful occurrence in his family, way back in the past, and that piece of timber in some way reminded him of it and brought the old sorrow home to him. He blinked three times, and asked, in a subdued tone:

"Is that iron-bark?"

Jack Bentley, the fluent liar of the party, caught his breath with a jerk and coughed, to cover the gasp and gain time. "I—iron-bark? Of course it is! I thought you would know iron-bark, mister." (Mister was silent.) "What else d'yer think it is?"

The dreamy, abstracted expression was back. The inspector, by-the-way, didn't know much about timber, but he had a great deal of instinct, and went by it when in doubt.

"L—look here, mister!" put in Dave Regan, in a tone of innocent puzzlement and with a blank bucolic face. "B—but don't the plans and specifications say iron-bark? Ours does, anyway. I—I'll git the papers from the tent and show yer, if yer like."

It was not necessary. The inspector admitted the fact slowly. He stooped, and with an absent air picked up a chip. He looked at it abstractedly for a moment, blinked his threefold blink; then, seeming to recollect an appointment, he woke up suddenly and asked briskly:

"Did this chip come off that girder?"

Blank silence. The inspector blinked six times, divided in threes, rapidly, mounted his horse, said "Day," and rode off.

Regan and party stared at each other.

"Wha—what did he do that for?" asked Andy Page, the third in the party.

"Do what for, you fool?" enquired Dave.

"Ta—take that chip for?"

"He's taking it to the office!" snarled Jack Bentley.

"What—what for? What does he want to do that for?"

"To get it blanky well analysed! You ass! Now are yer satisfied?" And Jack sat down hard on the timber, jerked out his pipe, and said to Dave, in a sharp, toothache tone:

"Gimmiamatch!"

"We—well! what are we to do now?" enquired Andy, who was the hardest grafter, but altogether helpless, hopeless, and useless in a crisis like this.

"Grain and varnish the bloomin' culvert!" snapped Bentley.

But Dave's eyes, that had been ruefully following the inspector, suddenly dilated. The inspector had ridden a short distance along the line, dismounted, thrown the bridle over a post, laid the chip (which was too big to go in his pocket) on top of it, got through the fence, and was now walking back at an angle across the line in the direction of the fencing party, who had worked up on the other side, a little more than opposite the culvert.

Dave took in the lay of the country at a glance and thought rapidly.

"Gimme an iron-bark chip!" he said suddenly.

Bentley, who was quick-witted when the track was shown him, as is a kangaroo dog (Jack ran by sight, not scent), glanced in the line of Dave's eyes, jumped up, and got a chip about the same size as that which the inspector had taken.

Now the "lay of the country" sloped generally to the line from both sides, and the angle between the inspector's horse, the fencing party, and the culvert was well within a clear concave space; but a couple of hundred yards back from the line and parallel to it (on the side on which Dave's party worked their timber) a fringe of scrub ran to within a few yards of a point which would be about in line with a single tree on the cleared slope, the horse, and the fencing party.

Dave took the iron-bark chip, ran along the bed of the water-course into the scrub, raced up the siding behind the bushes, got safely, though without breathing, across the exposed space, and brought the tree into line between him and the inspector, who was talking to the fencers. Then he began to work quickly down the slope towards the tree (which was a thin one), keeping it in line, his arms close to his sides, and working, as it were, down the trunk of the tree, as if the fencing party were kangaroos and Dave was trying to get a shot at them. The inspector, by-the-bye, had a habit of glancing now and then in the direction of his horse, as though under the impression that it was flighty and restless and inclined to bolt on opportunity. It was an anxious moment for all parties concerned—except the inspector. They didn't want HIM to be perturbed. And, just as Dave reached the foot of the tree, the inspector finished what he had to say to the fencers, turned, and started to walk briskly back to his horse. There was a thunderstorm coming. Now was the critical moment—there were certain prearranged signals between Dave's party and the fencers which might have interested the inspector, but none to meet a case like this.

Jack Bentley gasped, and started forward with an idea of intercepting the inspector and holding him for a few minutes in bogus conversation. Inspirations come to one at a critical moment, and it flashed on Jack's mind to send Andy instead. Andy looked as innocent and guileless as he was, but was uncomfortable in the vicinity of "funny business", and must have an honest excuse. "Not that that mattered," commented Jack afterwards; "it would have taken the inspector ten minutes to get at what Andy was driving at, whatever it was."

"Run, Andy! Tell him there's a heavy thunderstorm coming and he'd better stay in our humpy till it's over. Run! Don't stand staring like a blanky fool. He'll be gone!"

Andy started. But just then, as luck would have it, one of the fencers started after the inspector, hailing him as "Hi, mister!" He wanted to be set right about the survey or something—or to pretend to want to be set right—from motives of policy which I haven't time to explain here.

That fencer explained afterwards to Dave's party that he "seen what you coves was up to," and that's why he called the inspector back. But he told them that after they had told their yarn—which was a mistake.

"Come back, Andy!" cried Jack Bentley.

Dave Regan slipped round the tree, down on his hands and knees, and made quick time through the grass which, luckily, grew pretty tall on the thirty or forty yards of slope between the tree and the horse. Close to the horse, a thought struck Dave that pulled him up, and sent a shiver along his spine and a hungry feeling under it. The horse would break away and bolt! But the case was desperate. Dave ventured an interrogatory "Cope, cope, cope?" The horse turned its head wearily and regarded him with a mild eye, as if he'd expected him to come, and come on all fours, and wondered what had kept him so long; then he went on thinking. Dave reached the foot of the post; the horse obligingly leaning over on the other leg. Dave reared head and shoulders cautiously behind the post, like a snake; his hand went up twice, swiftly—the first time he grabbed the inspector's chip, and the second time he put the iron-bark one in its place. He drew down and back, and scuttled off for the tree like a gigantic tailless "goanna".

A few minutes later he walked up to the culvert from along the creek, smoking hard to settle his nerves.

The sky seemed to darken suddenly; the first great drops of the thunderstorm came pelting down. The inspector hurried to his horse, and cantered off along the line in the direction of the fettlers' camp.

He had forgotten all about the chip, and left it on top of the post!

Dave Regan sat down on the beam in the rain and swore comprehensively.

"Middleton's Peter"

I

The First Born

The struggling squatter is to be found in Australia as well as the "struggling farmer". The Australian squatter is not always the mighty wool king that English and American authors and other uninformed people apparently imagine him to be. Squatting, at the best, is but a game of chance. It depends mainly on the weather, and that, in New South Wales at least, depends on nothing.

Joe Middleton was a struggling squatter, with a station some distance to the westward of the furthest line reached by the ordinary "new chum". His run, at the time of our story, was only about six miles square, and his stock was limited in proportion. The hands on Joe's run consisted of his brother Dave, a middle-aged man known only as "Middleton's Peter" (who had been in the service of the Middleton family ever since Joe Middleton could remember), and an old black shepherd, with his gin and two boys.

It was in the first year of Joe's marriage. He had married a very ordinary girl, as far as Australian girls go, but in his eyes she was an angel. He really worshipped her.

One sultry afternoon in midsummer all the station hands, with the exception of Dave Middleton, were congregated about the homestead door, and it was evident from their solemn faces that something unusual was the matter. They appeared to be watching for something or someone across the flat, and the old black shepherd, who had been listening intently with bent head, suddenly straightened himself up and cried:

"I can hear the cart. I can see it!"

You must bear in mind that our blackfellows do not always talk the gibberish with which they are credited by story writers.

It was not until some time after Black Bill had spoken that the white—or, rather, the brown—portion of the party could see or even hear the approaching vehicle. At last, far out through the trunks of the native apple-trees, the cart was seen approaching; and as it came nearer it was evident that it was being driven at a break-neck pace, the horses cantering all the way, while the motion of the cart, as first one wheel and then the other sprang from a root or a rut, bore a striking resemblance to the Highland Fling. There were two persons in the cart. One was Mother Palmer, a stout, middle-aged party (who sometimes did the duties of a midwife), and the other was Dave Middleton, Joe's brother.

The cart was driven right up to the door with scarcely any abatement of speed, and was stopped so suddenly that Mrs. Palmer was sent sprawling on to the horse's rump. She was quickly helped down, and, as soon as she had recovered sufficient breath, she followed Black Mary into the bedroom where young Mrs. Middleton was lying, looking very pale and frightened. The horse which had been driven so cruelly had not done blowing before another cart appeared, also driven very fast. It contained old Mr. and Mrs. Middleton, who lived comfortably on a small farm not far from Palmer's place.

As soon as he had dumped Mrs. Palmer, Dave Middleton left the cart and, mounting a fresh horse which stood ready saddled in the yard, galloped off through the scrub in a different direction.

Half an hour afterwards Joe Middleton came home on a horse that had been almost ridden to death. His mother came out at the sound of his arrival, and he anxiously asked her:

"How is she?"

"Did you find Doc. Wild?" asked the mother.

"No, confound him!" exclaimed Joe bitterly. "He promised me faithfully to come over on Wednesday and stay until Maggie was right again. Now he has left Dean's and gone—Lord knows where. I suppose he is drinking again. How is Maggie?"

"It's all over now—the child is born. It's a boy; but she is very weak. Dave got Mrs. Palmer here just in time. I had better tell you at once that Mrs. Palmer says if we don't get a doctor here to-night poor Maggie won't live."

"Good God! and what am I to do?" cried Joe desperately.

"Is there any other doctor within reach?"

"No; there is only the one at B—; that's forty miles away, and he is laid up with the broken leg he got in the buggy accident. Where's Dave?"

"Gone to Black's shanty. One of Mrs. Palmer's sons thought he remembered someone saying that Doc. Wild was there last week. That's fifteen miles away."

"But it is our only hope," said Joe dejectedly. "I wish to God that I had taken Maggie to some civilised place a month ago."

Doc. Wild was a well-known character among the bushmen of New South Wales, and although the profession did not recognise him, and denounced him as an empiric, his skill was undoubted. Bushmen had great faith in him, and would often ride incredible distances in order to bring him to the bedside of a sick friend. He drank fearfully, but was seldom incapable of treating a patient; he would, however, sometimes be found in an obstinate mood and refuse to travel to the side of a sick person, and then the devil himself could not make the doctor budge. But for all this he was very generous—a fact that could, no doubt, be testified to by many a grateful sojourner in the lonely bush.

II

The Only Hope

Night came on, and still there was no change in the condition of the young wife, and no sign of the doctor. Several stockmen from the neighbouring stations, hearing that there was trouble at Joe Middleton's, had ridden over, and had galloped off on long, hopeless rides in search of a doctor. Being generally free from sickness themselves, these bushmen look upon it as a serious business even in its mildest form; what is more, their sympathy is always practical where it is possible for it to be so. One day, while out on the run after an "outlaw", Joe Middleton was badly thrown from his horse, and the break-neck riding that was done on that occasion from the time the horse came home with empty saddle until the rider was safe in bed and attended by a doctor was something extraordinary, even for the bush.

Before the time arrived when Dave Middleton might reasonably have been expected to return, the station people were anxiously watching for him, all except the old blackfellow and the two boys, who had gone to yard the sheep.

The party had been increased by Jimmy Nowlett, the bullocky, who had just arrived with a load of fencing wire and provisions for Middleton. Jimmy was standing in the moonlight, whip in hand, looking as anxious as the husband himself, and endeavouring to calculate by mental arithmetic the exact time it ought to take Dave to complete his double journey, taking into consideration the distance, the obstacles in the way, and the chances of horse-flesh.

But the time which Jimmy fixed for the arrival came without Dave.

Old Peter (as he was generally called, though he was not really old) stood aside in his usual sullen manner, his hat drawn down over his brow and eyes, and nothing visible but a thick and very horizontal black beard, from the depth of which emerged large clouds of very strong tobacco smoke, the product of a short, black, clay pipe.

They had almost given up all hope of seeing Dave return that night, when Peter slowly and deliberately removed his pipe and grunted:

"He's a-comin'."

He then replaced the pipe, and smoked on as before.

All listened, but not one of them could hear a sound.

"Yer ears must be pretty sharp for yer age, Peter. We can't hear him," remarked Jimmy Nowlett.

"His dog ken," said Peter.

The pipe was again removed and its abbreviated stem pointed in the direction of Dave's cattle dog, who had risen beside his kennel with pointed ears, and was looking eagerly in the direction from which his master was expected to come.

Presently the sound of horse's hoofs was distinctly heard.

"I can hear two horses," cried Jimmy Nowlett excitedly.

"There's only one," said old Peter quietly.

A few moments passed, and a single horseman appeared on the far side of the flat.

"It's Doc. Wild on Dave's horse," cried Jimmy Nowlett. "Dave don't ride like that."

"It's Dave," said Peter, replacing his pipe and looking more unsociable than ever.

Dave rode up and, throwing himself wearily from the saddle, stood ominously silent by the side of his horse.

Joe Middleton said nothing, but stood aside with an expression of utter hopelessness on his face.

"Not there?" asked Jimmy Nowlett at last, addressing Dave.

"Yes, he's there," answered Dave, impatiently.

This was not the answer they expected, but nobody seemed surprised.

"Drunk?" asked Jimmy.

"Yes."

Here old Peter removed his pipe, and pronounced the one word—"How?"

"What the hell do you mean by that?" muttered Dave, whose patience had evidently been severely tried by the clever but intemperate bush doctor.

"How drunk?" explained Peter, with great equanimity.

"Stubborn drunk, blind drunk, beastly drunk, dead drunk, and damned well drunk, if that's what you want to know!"

"What did Doc. say?" asked Jimmy.

"Said he was sick—had lumbago—wouldn't come for the Queen of England; said he wanted a course of treatment himself. Curse him! I have no patience to talk about him."

"I'd give him a course of treatment," muttered Jimmy viciously, trailing the long lash of his bullock-whip through the grass and spitting spitefully at the ground.

Dave turned away and joined Joe, who was talking earnestly to his mother by the kitchen door. He told them that he had spent an hour trying to persuade Doc. Wild to come, and, that before he had left the shanty, Black had promised him faithfully to bring the doctor over as soon as his obstinate mood wore off.

Just then a low moan was heard from the sick room, followed by the sound of Mother Palmer's voice calling old Mrs. Middleton, who went inside immediately.

No one had noticed the disappearance of Peter, and when he presently returned from the stockyard, leading the only fresh horse that remained, Jimmy Nowlett began to regard him with some interest. Peter transferred the saddle from Dave's horse to the other, and then went into a small room off the kitchen, which served him as a bedroom; from it he soon returned with a formidable-looking revolver, the chambers of which he examined in the moonlight in full view of all the company. They thought for a moment the man had gone mad. Old Middleton leaped quickly behind Nowlett, and Black Mary, who had come out to the cask at the corner for a dipper of water, dropped the dipper and was inside like a shot. One of the black boys came softly up at that moment; as soon as his sharp eye "spotted" the weapon, he disappeared as though the earth had swallowed him.

"What the mischief are yer goin' ter do, Peter?" asked Jimmy.

"Goin' to fetch him," said Peter, and, after carefully emptying his pipe and replacing it in a leather pouch at his belt, he mounted and rode off at an easy canter.

Jimmy watched the horse until it disappeared at the edge of the flat, and then after coiling up the long lash of his bullock-whip in the dust until it looked like a sleeping snake, he prodded the small end of the long pine handle into the middle of the coil, as though driving home a point, and said in a tone of intense conviction:

"He'll fetch him."

III

Doc. Wild

Peter gradually increased his horse's speed along the rough bush track until he was riding at a good pace. It was ten miles to the main road, and five from there to the shanty kept by Black.

For some time before Peter started the atmosphere had been very close and oppressive. The great black edge of a storm-cloud had risen in the east, and everything indicated the approach of a thunderstorm. It was not long coming. Before Peter had completed six miles of his journey, the clouds rolled over, obscuring the moon, and an Australian thunderstorm came on with its mighty downpour, its blinding lightning, and its earth-shaking thunder. Peter rode steadily on, only pausing now and then until a flash revealed the track in front of him.

Black's shanty—or, rather, as the sign had it, "Post Office and General Store"—was, as we have said, five miles along the main road from the point where Middleton's track joined it. The building was of the usual style of bush architecture. About two hundred yards nearer the creek, which crossed the road further on, stood a large bark and slab stable, large enough to have met the requirements of a legitimate bush "public".

The reader may doubt that a "sly grog shop" could openly carry on business on a main Government road along which mounted troopers were continually passing. But then, you see, mounted troopers get thirsty like other men; moreover, they could always get their thirst quenched 'gratis' at these places; so the reader will be prepared to hear that on this very night two troopers' horses were stowed snugly away in the stable, and two troopers were stowed snugly away in the back room of the shanty, sleeping off the effects of their cheap but strong potations.

There were two rooms, of a sort, attached to the stables—one at each end. One was occupied by a man who was "generally useful", and the other was the surgery, office, and bedroom 'pro tem.' of Doc. Wild.

Doc. Wild was a tall man, of spare proportions. He had a cadaverous face, black hair, bushy black eyebrows, eagle nose, and eagle eyes. He never slept while he was drinking. On this occasion he sat in front of the fire on a low three-legged stool. His knees were drawn up, his toes hooked round the front legs of the stool, one hand resting on one knee, and one elbow (the hand supporting the chin) resting on the other. He was staring intently into the fire, on which an old black saucepan was boiling and sending forth a pungent odour of herbs. There seemed something uncanny about the doctor as the red light of the fire fell on his hawk-like face and gleaming eyes. He might have been Mephistopheles watching some infernal brew.

He had sat there some time without stirring a finger, when the door suddenly burst open and Middleton's Peter stood within, dripping wet. The doctor turned his black, piercing eyes upon the intruder (who regarded him silently) for a moment, and then asked quietly:

"What the hell do you want?"

"I want you," said Peter.

"And what do you want me for?"

"I want you to come to Joe Middleton's wife. She's bad," said Peter calmly.

"I won't come," shouted the doctor. "I've brought enough horse-stealers into the world already. If any more want to come they can go to blazes for me. Now, you get out of this!"

"Don't get yer rag out," said Peter quietly. "The hoss-stealer's come, an' nearly killed his mother ter begin with; an' if yer don't get yer physic-box an' come wi' me, by the great God I'll—"

Here the revolver was produced and pointed at Doc. Wild's head. The sight of the weapon had a sobering effect upon the doctor. He rose, looked at Peter critically for a moment, knocked the weapon out of his hand, and said slowly and deliberately:

"Wall, ef the case es as serious as that, I (hic) reckon I'd better come."

Peter was still of the same opinion, so Doc. Wild proceeded to get his medicine chest ready. He explained afterwards, in one of his softer moments, that the shooter didn't frighten him so much as it touched his memory—"sorter put him in mind of the old days in California, and made him think of the man he might have been," he'd say,—"kinder touched his heart and slid the durned old panorama in front of him like a flash; made him think of the time when he slipped three leaden pills into 'Blue Shirt' for winking at a new chum behind his (the Doc.'s) back when he was telling a truthful yarn, and charged the said 'Blue Shirt' a hundred dollars for extracting the said pills."

Joe Middleton's wife is a grandmother now.

Peter passed after the manner of his sort; he was found dead in his bunk.

Poor Doc. Wild died in a shepherd's hut at the Dry Creeks. The shepherds (white men) found him, "naked as he was born and with the hide half burned off him with the sun," rounding up imaginary snakes on a dusty clearing, one blazing hot day. The hut-keeper had some "quare" (queer) experiences with the doctor during the next three days and used, in after years, to tell of them, between the puffs of his pipe, calmly and solemnly and as if the story was rather to the doctor's credit than otherwise. The shepherds sent for the police and a doctor, and sent word to Joe Middleton. Doc. Wild was sensible towards the end. His interview with the other doctor was characteristic. "And, now you see how far I am," he said in conclusion—"have you brought the brandy?" The other doctor had. Joe Middleton came with his waggonette, and in it the softest mattress and pillows the station afforded. He also, in his innocence, brought a dozen of soda-water. Doc. Wild took Joe's hand feebly, and, a little later, he "passed out" (as he would have said) murmuring "something that sounded like poetry", in an unknown tongue. Joe took the body to the home station. "Who's the boss bringin'?" asked the shearers, seeing the waggonette coming very slowly and the boss walking by the horses' heads. "Doc. Wild," said a station hand. "Take yer hats off."

They buried him with bush honours, and chiselled his name on a slab of bluegum—a wood that lasts.

The Mystery of Dave Regan

"And then there was Dave Regan," said the traveller. "Dave used to die oftener than any other bushman I knew. He was always being reported dead and turnin' up again. He seemed to like it—except once, when his brother drew his money and drank it all to drown his grief at what he called Dave's 'untimely end'. Well, Dave went up to Queensland once with cattle, and was away three years and reported dead, as usual. He was drowned in the Bogan this time while tryin' to swim his horse acrost a flood—and his sweetheart hurried up and got spliced to a worse man before Dave got back.

"Well, one day I was out in the bush lookin' for timber, when the biggest storm ever knowed in that place come on. There was hail in it, too, as big as bullets, and if I hadn't got behind a stump and crouched down in time I'd have been riddled like a—like a bushranger. As it was, I got soakin' wet. The storm was over in a few minutes, the water run off down the gullies, and the sun come out and the scrub steamed—and stunk like a new pair of moleskin trousers. I went on along the track, and presently I seen a long, lanky chap get on to a long, lanky horse and ride out of a bush yard at the edge of a clearin'. I knowed it was Dave d'reckly I set eyes on him.

"Dave used to ride a tall, holler-backed thoroughbred with a body and limbs like a kangaroo dog, and it would circle around you and sidle away as if it was frightened you was goin' to jab a knife into it.

""'Ello! Dave!' said I, as he came spurrin' up. 'How are yer!'

""'Ello, Jim!' says he. 'How are you?'

"'All right!' says I. 'How are yer gettin' on?'

"But, before we could say any more, that horse shied away and broke off through the scrub to the right. I waited, because I knowed Dave would come back again if I waited long enough; and in about ten minutes he came sidlin' in from the scrub to the left.

"'Oh, I'm all right,' says he, spurrin' up sideways; 'How are you?'

"'Right!' says I. 'How's the old people?'

"'Oh, I ain't been home yet,' says he, holdin' out his hand; but, afore I could grip it, the cussed horse sidled off to the south end of the clearin' and broke away again through the scrub.

"I heard Dave swearin' about the country for twenty minutes or so, and then he came spurrin' and cursin' in from the other end of the clearin'.

"'Where have you been all this time?' I said, as the horse came curvin' up like a boomerang.

"'Gulf country,' said Dave.

"'That was a storm, Dave,' said I.

"'My oath!' says Dave.

"'Get caught in it?'

"'Yes.'

"'Got to shelter?'

"'No.'

"'But you're as dry's a bone, Dave!'

"Dave grinned. '—and—and—the—!' he yelled.

"He said that to the horse as it boomeranged off again and broke away through the scrub. I waited; but he didn't come back, and I reckoned he'd got so far away before he could pull up that he didn't think it worth while comin' back; so I went on. By-and-bye I got thinkin'. Dave was as dry as a bone, and I knowed that he hadn't had time to get to shelter, for there wasn't a shed within twelve miles. He wasn't only dry, but his coat was creased and dusty too—same as if he'd been sleepin' in a holler log; and when I come to think of it, his face seemed thinner and whiter than it used ter, and so did his hands and wrists, which always stuck a long way out of his coat-sleeves; and there was blood on his face—but I thought he'd got scratched with a twig. (Dave used to wear a coat three or four sizes too small for him, with sleeves that didn't come much below his elbows and a tail that scarcely reached his waist behind.) And his hair seemed dark and lank, instead of bein' sandy and stickin' out like an old fibre brush, as it used ter. And then I thought his voice sounded different, too. And, when I enquired next day, there was no one heard of Dave, and the chaps reckoned I must have been drunk, or seen his ghost.

"It didn't seem all right at all—it worried me a lot. I couldn't make out how Dave kept dry; and the horse and saddle and saddle-cloth was wet. I told the chaps how he talked to me and what he said, and how he swore at the horse; but they only said it was Dave's ghost and nobody else's. I told 'em about him bein' dry as a bone after gettin' caught in that storm; but they only laughed and said it was a dry place where Dave went to. I talked and argued about it until the chaps began to tap their foreheads and wink—then I left off talking. But I didn't leave off thinkin'—I always hated a mystery. Even Dave's father told me that Dave couldn't be alive or else his ghost wouldn't be round—he said he knew Dave better than that. One or two fellers did turn up afterwards that had seen Dave about the time that I did—and then the chaps said they was sure that Dave was dead.

"But one fine day, as a lot of us chaps was playin' pitch and toss at the shanty, one of the fellers yelled out:

"'By Gee! Here comes Dave Regan!'

"And I looked up and saw Dave himself, sidlin' out of a cloud of dust on a long lanky horse. He rode into the stockyard, got down, hung his horse up to a post, put up the rails, and then come slopin' towards us with a half-acre grin on his face. Dave had long, thin bow-legs, and when he was on the ground he moved as if he was on roller skates.

""'El-lo, Dave!' says I. 'How are yer?'

""'Ello, Jim!' said he. 'How the blazes are you?'

"'All right!' says I, shakin' hands. 'How are yer?'

"'Oh! I'm all right!' he says. 'How are yer poppin' up!'

"Well, when we'd got all that settled, and the other chaps had asked how he was, he said: 'Ah, well! Let's have a drink.'

"And all the other chaps crawfished up and flung themselves round the corner and sidled into the bar after Dave. We had a lot of talk, and he told us that he'd been down before, but had gone away without seein' any of us, except me, because he'd suddenly heard of a mob of cattle at a station two hundred miles away; and after a while I took him aside and said:

"'Look here, Dave! Do you remember the day I met you after the storm?'

"He scratched his head.

"'Why, yes,' he says.

"'Did you get under shelter that day?'

"'Why—no.'

"'Then how the blazes didn't yer get wet?'

"Dave grinned; then he says:

"'Why, when I seen the storm coming I took off me clothes and stuck 'em in a holler log till the rain was over.'

"'Yes,' he says, after the other coves had done laughin', but before I'd done thinking; 'I kept my clothes dry and got a good refreshin' shower-bath into the bargain.'

"Then he scratched the back of his neck with his little finger, and dropped his jaw, and thought a bit; then he rubbed the top of his head and his shoulder, reflective-like, and then he said:

"'But I didn't reckon for them there blanky hailstones.'"

"I suppose your wife will be glad to see you," said Mitchell to his mate in their camp by the dam at Hungerford. They were overhauling their swags, and throwing away the blankets, and calico, and old clothes, and rubbish they didn't want—everything, in fact, except their pocket-books and letters and portraits, things which men carry about with them always, that are found on them when they die, and sent to their relations if possible. Otherwise they are taken in charge by the constable who officiates at the inquest, and forwarded to the Minister of Justice along with the depositions.

It was the end of the shearing season. Mitchell and his mate had been lucky enough to get two good sheds in succession, and were going to take the coach from Hungerford to Bourke on their way to Sydney. The morning stars were bright yet, and they sat down to a final billy of tea, two dusty Johnny-cakes, and a scrag of salt mutton.

"Yes," said Mitchell's mate, "and I'll be glad to see her too."

"I suppose you will," said Mitchell. He placed his pint-pot between his feet, rested his arm against his knee, and stirred the tea meditatively with the handle of his pocket-knife. It was vaguely understood that Mitchell had been married at one period of his chequered career.

"I don't think we ever understood women properly," he said, as he took a cautious sip to see if his tea was cool and sweet enough, for his lips were sore; "I don't think we ever will—we never took the trouble to try, and if we did it would be only wasted brain power that might just as well be spent on the blackfellow's lingo; because by the time you've learnt it they'll be extinct, and woman 'll be extinct before you've learnt her.... The morning star looks bright, doesn't it?"

"Ah, well," said Mitchell after a while, "there's many little things we might try to understand women in. I read in a piece of newspaper the other day about how a man changes after he's married; how he gets short, and impatient, and bored (which is only natural), and sticks up a wall of newspaper between himself and his wife when he's at home; and how it comes like a cold shock to her, and all her air-castles vanish, and in the end she often thinks about taking the baby and the clothes she stands in, and going home for sympathy and comfort to mother.

"Perhaps she never got a word of sympathy from her mother in her life, nor a day's comfort at home before she was married; but that doesn't make the slightest difference. It doesn't make any difference in your case either, if you haven't been acting like a dutiful son-in-law.

"Somebody wrote that a woman's love is her whole existence, while a man's love is only part of his—which is true, and only natural and reasonable, all things considered. But women never consider as a rule. A man can't go on talking lovey-dovey talk for ever, and listening to his young wife's prattle when he's got to think about making a living, and nursing her and answering her childish questions and telling her he loves his little ownest every minute in the day, while the bills are running up, and rent mornings begin to fly round and hustle and crowd him.

"He's got her and he's satisfied; and if the truth is known he loves her really more than he did when they were engaged, only she won't be satisfied about it unless he tells her so every hour in the day. At least that's how it is for the first few months.

"But a woman doesn't understand these things—she never will, she can't—and it would be just as well for us to try and understand that she doesn't and can't understand them."

Mitchell knocked the tea-leaves out of his pannikin against his boot, and reached for the billy.

"There's many little things we might do that seem mere trifles and nonsense to us, but mean a lot to her; that wouldn't be any trouble or sacrifice to us, but might help to make her life happy. It's just because we never think about these little things—don't think them worth thinking about, in fact—they never enter our intellectual foreheads.

"For instance, when you're going out in the morning you might put your arms round her and give her a hug and a kiss, without her having to remind you. You may forget about it and never think any more of it—but she will.

"It wouldn't be any trouble to you, and would only take a couple of seconds, and would give her something to be happy about when you're gone, and make her sing to herself for hours while she bustles about her work and thinks up what she'll get you for dinner."

Mitchell's mate sighed, and shifted the sugar-bag over towards Mitchell. He seemed touched and bothered over something.

"Then again," said Mitchell, "it mightn't be convenient for you to go home to dinner—something might turn up during the morning—you might have some important business to do, or meet some chaps and get invited to lunch and not be very well able to refuse, when it's too late, or you haven't a chance to send a message to your wife. But then again, chaps and business seem very big things to you, and only little things to the wife; just as lovey-dovey talk is important to her and nonsense to you. And when you come to analyse it, one is not so big, nor the other so small, after all; especially when you come to think that chaps can always wait, and business is only an inspiration in your mind, nine cases out of ten.

"Think of the trouble she takes to get you a good dinner, and how she keeps it hot between two plates in the oven, and waits hour after hour till the dinner gets dried up, and all her morning's work is wasted. Think how it hurts her, and how anxious she'll be (especially if you're inclined to booze) for fear that something has happened to you. You can't get it out of the heads of some young wives that you're liable to get run over, or knocked down, or assaulted, or robbed, or get into one of the fixes that a woman is likely to get into. But about the dinner waiting. Try and put yourself in her place. Wouldn't you get mad under the same circumstances? I know I would.

"I remember once, only just after I was married, I was invited unexpectedly to a kidney pudding and beans—which was my favourite grub at the time—and I didn't resist, especially as it was washing day and I told the wife not to bother about anything for dinner. I got home an hour or so late, and had a good explanation thought out, when the wife met me with a smile as if we had just been left a thousand pounds. She'd got her washing finished without assistance, though I'd told her to get somebody to help her, and she had a kidney pudding and beans, with a lot of extras thrown in, as a pleasant surprise for me.

"Well, I kissed her, and sat down, and stuffed till I thought every mouthful would choke me. I got through with it somehow, but I've never cared for kidney pudding or beans since."

Mitchell felt for his pipe with a fatherly smile in his eyes.

"And then again," he continued, as he cut up his tobacco, "your wife might put on a new dress and fix herself up and look well, and you might think so and be satisfied with her appearance and be proud to take her out; but you want to tell her so, and tell her so as often as you think about it—and try to think a little oftener than men usually do, too."

"You should have made a good husband, Jack," said his mate, in a softened tone.

"Ah, well, perhaps I should," said Mitchell, rubbing up his tobacco; then he asked abstractedly: "What sort of a husband did you make, Joe?"

"I might have made a better one than I did," said Joe seriously, and rather bitterly, "but I know one thing, I'm going to try and make up for it when I go back this time."

"We all say that," said Mitchell reflectively, filling his pipe. "She loves you, Joe."

"I know she does," said Joe.

Mitchell lit up.

"And so would any man who knew her or had seen her letters to you," he said between the puffs. "She's happy and contented enough, I believe?"

"Yes," said Joe, "at least while I was there. She's never easy when I'm away. I might have made her a good deal more happy and contented without hurting myself much."

Mitchell smoked long, soft, measured puffs.

His mate shifted uneasily and glanced at him a couple of times, and seemed to become impatient, and to make up his mind about something; or perhaps he got an idea that Mitchell had been "having" him, and felt angry over being betrayed into maudlin confidences; for he asked abruptly:

"How is your wife now, Mitchell?"

"I don't know," said Mitchell calmly.

"Don't know?" echoed the mate. "Didn't you treat her well?"

Mitchell removed his pipe and drew a long breath.

"Ah, well, I tried to," he said wearily.

"Well, did you put your theory into practice?"

"I did," said Mitchell very deliberately.

Joe waited, but nothing came.

"Well?" he asked impatiently, "How did it act? Did it work well?"

"I don't know," said Mitchell (puff); "she left me."

"What!"

Mitchell jerked the half-smoked pipe from his mouth, and rapped the burning tobacco out against the toe of his boot.

"She left me," he said, standing up and stretching himself. Then, with a vicious jerk of his arm, "She left me for—another kind of a fellow!"

He looked east towards the public-house, where they were taking the coach-horses from the stable.

"Why don't you finish your tea, Joe? The billy's getting cold."

Mitchell on Women

"All the same," said Mitchell's mate, continuing an argument by the camp-fire; "all the same, I think that a woman can stand cold water better than a man. Why, when I was staying in a boarding-house in Dunedin, one very cold winter, there was a lady lodger who went down to the shower-bath first thing every morning; never missed one; sometimes went in freezing weather when I wouldn't go into a cold bath for a fiver; and sometimes she'd stay under the shower for ten minutes at a time."

"How'd you know?"

"Why, my room was near the bath-room, and I could hear the shower and tap going, and her floundering about."

"Hear your grandmother!" exclaimed Mitchell, contemptuously. "You don't know women yet. Was this woman married? Did she have a husband there?"

"No; she was a young widow."

"Ah! well, it would have been the same if she was a young girl—or an old one. Were there some passable men-boarders there?"

"I was there."

"Oh, yes! But I mean, were there any there beside you?"

"Oh, yes, there were three or four; there was—a clerk and a—"

"Never mind, as long as there was something with trousers on. Did it ever strike you that she never got into the bath at all?"

"Why, no! What would she want to go there at all for, in that case?"

"To make an impression on the men," replied Mitchell promptly. "She wanted to make out she was nice, and wholesome, and well-washed, and particular. Made an impression on YOU, it seems, or you wouldn't remember it."

"Well, yes, I suppose so; and, now I come to think of it, the bath didn't seem to injure her make-up or wet her hair; but I supposed she held her head from under the shower somehow."

"Did she make-up so early in the morning?" asked Mitchell.

"Yes—I'm sure."

"That's unusual; but it might have been so where there was a lot of boarders. And about the hair—that didn't count for anything, because washing-the-head ain't supposed to be always included in a lady's bath; it's only supposed to be washed once a fortnight, and some don't do it once a month. The hair takes so long to dry; it don't matter so much if the woman's got short, scraggy hair; but if a girl's hair was down to her waist it would take hours to dry."

"Well, how do they manage it without wetting their heads?"

"Oh, that's easy enough. They have a little oilskin cap that fits tight over the forehead, and they put it on, and bunch their hair up in it when they go under the shower. Did you ever see a woman sit in a sunny place with her hair down after having a wash?"

"Yes, I used to see one do that regular where I was staying; but I thought she only did it to show off."

"Not at all—she was drying her hair; though perhaps she was showing off at the same time, for she wouldn't sit where you—or even a Chinaman—could see her, if she didn't think she had a good head of hair. Now, I'LL tell you a yarn about a woman's bath. I was stopping at a shabby-genteel boarding-house in Melbourne once, and one very cold winter, too; and there was a rather good-looking woman there, looking for a husband. She used to go down to the bath every morning, no matter how cold it was, and flounder and splash about as if she enjoyed it, till you'd feel as though you'd like to go and catch hold of her and wrap her in a rug and carry her in to the fire and nurse her till she was warm again."

Mitchell's mate moved uneasily, and crossed the other leg; he seemed greatly interested.

"But she never went into the water at all!" continued Mitchell. "As soon as one or two of the men was up in the morning she'd come down from her room in a dressing-gown. It was a toney dressing-gown, too, and set her off properly. She knew how to dress, anyway; most of that sort of women do. The gown was a kind of green colour, with pink and white flowers all over it, and red lining, and a lot of coffee-coloured lace round the neck and down the front. Well, she'd come tripping downstairs and along the passage, holding up one side of the gown to show her little bare white foot in a slipper; and in the other hand she carried her tooth-brush and bath-brush, and soap—like this—so's we all could see 'em; trying to make out she was too particular to use soap after anyone else. She could afford to buy her own soap, anyhow; it was hardly ever wet.

"Well, she'd go into the bathroom and turn on the tap and shower; when she got about three inches of water in the bath, she'd step in, holding up her gown out of the water, and go slithering and kicking up and down the bath, like this, making a tremendous splashing. Of course she'd turn off the shower first, and screw it off very tight—wouldn't do to let that leak, you know; she might get wet; but she'd leave the other tap on, so as to make all the more noise."

"But how did you come to know all about this?"

"Oh, the servant girl told me. One morning she twigged her through a corner of the bathroom window that the curtain didn't cover."

"You seem to have been pretty thick with servant girls."

"So do you with landladies! But never mind—let me finish the yarn. When she thought she'd splashed enough, she'd get out, wipe her feet, wash her face and hands, and carefully unbutton the two top buttons of her gown; then throw a towel over her head and shoulders, and listen at the door till she thought she heard some of the men moving about. Then she'd start for her room, and, if she met one of the men-boarders in the passage or on the stairs, she'd drop her eyes, and pretend to see for the first time that the top of her dressing-gown wasn't buttoned—and she'd give a little start and grab the gown and scurry off to her room buttoning it up.

"And sometimes she'd come skipping into the breakfast-room late, looking awfully sweet in her dressing-gown; and if she saw any of us there, she'd pretend to be much startled, and say that she thought all the men had gone out, and make as though she was going to clear; and someone 'd jump up and give her a chair, while someone else said, 'Come in, Miss Brown! come in! Don't let us frighten you. Come right in, and have your breakfast before it gets cold.' So she'd flutter a bit in pretty confusion, and then make a sweet little girly-girly dive for her chair, and tuck her feet away under the table; and she'd blush, too, but I don't know how she managed that.

"I know another trick that women have; it's mostly played by private barmaids. That is, to leave a stocking by accident in the bathroom for the gentlemen to find. If the barmaid's got a nice foot and ankle, she uses one of her own stockings; but if she hasn't she gets hold of a stocking that belongs to a girl that has. Anyway, she'll have one readied up somehow. The stocking must be worn and nicely darned; one that's been worn will keep the shape of the leg and foot—at least till it's washed again. Well, the barmaid generally knows what time the gentlemen go to bath, and she'll make it a point of going down just as a gentleman's going. Of course he'll give her the preference—let her go first, you know—and she'll go in and accidentally leave the stocking in a place where he's sure to see it, and when she comes out he'll go in and find it; and very likely he'll be a jolly sort of fellow, and when they're all sitting down to breakfast he'll come in and ask them to guess what he's found, and then he'll hold up the stocking. The barmaid likes this sort of thing; but she'll hold down her head, and pretend to be confused, and keep her eyes on her plate, and there'll be much blushing and all that sort of thing, and perhaps she'll gammon to be mad at him, and the landlady'll say, 'Oh, Mr. Smith! how can yer? At the breakfast table, too!' and they'll all laugh and look at the barmaid, and she'll get more embarrassed than ever, and spill her tea, and make out as though the stocking didn't belong to her."

No Place for a Woman

He had a selection on a long box-scrub siding of the ridges, about half a mile back and up from the coach road. There were no neighbours that I ever heard of, and the nearest "town" was thirty miles away. He grew wheat among the stumps of his clearing, sold the crop standing to a Cockie who lived ten miles away, and had some surplus sons; or, some seasons, he reaped it by hand, had it thrashed by travelling "steamer" (portable steam engine and machine), and carried the grain, a few bags at a time, into the mill on his rickety dray.

He had lived alone for upwards of 15 years, and was known to those who knew him as "Ratty Howlett".

Trav'lers and strangers failed to see anything uncommonly ratty about him. It was known, or, at least, it was believed, without question, that while at work he kept his horse saddled and bridled, and hung up to the fence, or grazing about, with the saddle on—or, anyway, close handy for a moment's notice—and whenever he caught sight, over the scrub and through the quarter-mile break in it, of a traveller on the road, he would jump on his horse and make after him. If it was a horseman he usually pulled him up inside of a mile. Stories were told of unsuccessful chases, misunderstandings, and complications arising out of Howlett's mania for running down and bailing up travellers. Sometimes he caught one every day for a week, sometimes not one for weeks—it was a lonely track.

The explanation was simple, sufficient, and perfectly natural—from a bushman's point of view. Ratty only wanted to have a yarn. He and the traveller would camp in the shade for half an hour or so and yarn and smoke. The old man would find out where the traveller came from, and how long he'd been there, and where he was making for, and how long he reckoned he'd be away; and ask if there had been any rain along the traveller's back track, and how the country looked after the drought; and he'd get the traveller's ideas on abstract questions—if he had any. If it was a footman (swagman), and he was short of tobacco, old Howlett always had half a stick ready for him. Sometimes, but very rarely, he'd invite the swagman back to the hut for a pint of tea, or a bit of meat, flour, tea, or sugar, to carry him along the track.

And, after the yarn by the road, they said, the old man would ride back, refreshed, to his lonely selection, and work on into the night as long as he could see his solitary old plough horse, or the scoop of his long-handled shovel.

And so it was that I came to make his acquaintance—or, rather, that he made mine. I was cantering easily along the track—I was making for the north-west with a pack horse—when about a mile beyond the track to the selection I heard, "Hi, Mister!" and saw a dust cloud following me. I had heard of "Old Ratty Howlett" casually, and so was prepared for him.

A tall gaunt man on a little horse. He was clean-shaven, except for a frill beard round under his chin, and his long wavy, dark hair was turning grey; a square, strong-faced man, and reminded me of one full-faced portrait of Gladstone more than any other face I had seen. He had large reddish-brown eyes, deep set under heavy eyebrows, and with something of the blackfellow in them—the sort of eyes that will peer at something on the horizon that no one else can see. He had a way of talking to the horizon, too—more than to his companion; and he had a deep vertical wrinkle in his forehead that no smile could lessen.

I got down and got out my pipe, and we sat on a log and yarned awhile on bush subjects; and then, after a pause, he shifted uneasily, it seemed to me, and asked rather abruptly, and in an altered tone, if I was married. A queer question to ask a traveller; more especially in my case, as I was little more than a boy then.

He talked on again of old things and places where we had both been, and asked after men he knew, or had known—drovers and others—and whether they were living yet. Most of his inquiries went back before my time; but some of the drovers, one or two overlanders with whom he had been mates in his time, had grown old into mine, and I knew them. I notice now, though I didn't then—and if I had it would not have seemed strange from a bush point of view—that he didn't ask for news, nor seem interested in it.

Then after another uneasy pause, during which he scratched crosses in the dust with a stick, he asked me, in the same queer tone and without looking at me or looking up, if I happened to know anything about doctoring—if I'd ever studied it.

I asked him if anyone was sick at his place. He hesitated, and said "No." Then I wanted to know why he had asked me that question, and he was so long about answering that I began to think he was hard of hearing, when, at last, he muttered something about my face reminding him of a young fellow he knew of who'd gone to Sydney to "study for a doctor". That might have been, and looked natural enough; but why didn't he ask me straight out if I was the chap he "knowed of"? Travellers do not like beating about the bush in conversation.

He sat in silence for a good while, with his arms folded, and looking absently away over the dead level of the great scrubs that spread from the foot of the ridge we were on to where a blue peak or two of a distant range showed above the bush on the horizon.

I stood up and put my pipe away and stretched. Then he seemed to wake up. "Better come back to the hut and have a bit of dinner," he said. "The missus will about have it ready, and I'll spare you a handful of hay for the horses."

The hay decided it. It was a dry season. I was surprised to hear of a wife, for I thought he was a hatter—I had always heard so; but perhaps I had been mistaken, and he had married lately; or had got a housekeeper. The farm was an irregularly-shaped clearing in the scrub, with a good many stumps in it, with a broken-down two-rail fence along the frontage, and logs and "dog-leg" the rest. It was about as lonely-looking a place as I had seen, and I had seen some out-of-the-way, God-forgotten holes where men lived alone. The hut was in the top corner, a two-roomed slab hut, with a shingle roof, which must have been uncommon round there in the days when that hut was built. I was used to bush carpentering, and saw that the place had been put up by a man who had plenty of life and hope in front of him, and for someone else beside himself. But there were two unfinished skilling rooms built on to the back of the hut; the posts, sleepers, and wall-plates had been well put up and fitted, and the slab walls were up, but the roof had never been put on. There was nothing but burrs and nettles inside those walls, and an old wooden bullock plough and a couple of yokes were dry-rotting across the back doorway. The remains of a straw-stack, some hay under a bark humpy, a small iron plough, and an old stiff coffin-headed grey draught horse, were all that I saw about the place.

But there was a bit of a surprise for me inside, in the shape of a clean white tablecloth on the rough slab table which stood on stakes driven into the ground. The cloth was coarse, but it was a tablecloth—not a spare sheet put on in honour of unexpected visitors—and perfectly clean. The tin plates, pannikins, and jam tins that served as sugar bowls and salt cellars were polished brightly. The walls and fireplace were whitewashed, the clay floor swept, and clean sheets of newspaper laid on the slab mantleshelf under the row of biscuit tins that held the groceries. I thought that his wife, or housekeeper, or whatever she was, was a clean and tidy woman about a house. I saw no woman; but on the sofa—a light, wooden, batten one, with runged arms at the ends—lay a woman's dress on a lot of sheets of old stained and faded newspapers. He looked at it in a puzzled way, knitting his forehead, then took it up absently and folded it. I saw then that it was a riding skirt and jacket. He bundled them into the newspapers and took them into the bedroom.

"The wife was going on a visit down the creek this afternoon," he said rapidly and without looking at me, but stooping as if to have another look through the door at those distant peaks. "I suppose she got tired o' waitin', and went and took the daughter with her. But, never mind, the grub is ready." There was a camp-oven with a leg of mutton and potatoes sizzling in it on the hearth, and billies hanging over the fire. I noticed the billies had been scraped, and the lids polished.

There seemed to be something queer about the whole business, but then he and his wife might have had a "breeze" during the morning. I thought so during the meal, when the subject of women came up, and he said one never knew how to take a woman, etc.; but there was nothing in what he said that need necessarily have referred to his wife or to any woman in particular. For the rest he talked of old bush things, droving, digging, and old bushranging—but never about live things and living men, unless any of the old mates he talked about happened to be alive by accident. He was very restless in the house, and never took his hat off.

There was a dress and a woman's old hat hanging on the wall near the door, but they looked as if they might have been hanging there for a lifetime. There seemed something queer about the whole place—something wanting; but then all out-of-the-way bush homes are haunted by that something wanting, or, more likely, by the spirits of the things that should have been there, but never had been.

As I rode down the track to the road I looked back and saw old Howlett hard at work in a hole round a big stump with his long-handled shovel.

I'd noticed that he moved and walked with a slight list to port, and put his hand once or twice to the small of his back, and I set it down to lumbago, or something of that sort.

Up in the Never Never I heard from a drover who had known Howlett that his wife had died in the first year, and so this mysterious woman, if she was his wife, was, of course, his second wife. The drover seemed surprised and rather amused at the thought of old Howlett going in for matrimony again.

I rode back that way five years later, from the Never Never. It was early in the morning—I had ridden since midnight. I didn't think the old man would be up and about; and, besides, I wanted to get on home, and have a look at the old folk, and the mates I'd left behind—and the girl. But I hadn't got far past the point where Howlett's track joined the road, when I happened to look back, and saw him on horseback, stumbling down the track. I waited till he came up.

He was riding the old grey draught horse this time, and it looked very much broken down. I thought it would have come down every step, and fallen like an old rotten humpy in a gust of wind. And the old man was not much better off. I saw at once that he was a very sick man. His face was drawn, and he bent forward as if he was hurt. He got down stiffly and awkwardly, like a hurt man, and as soon as his feet touched the ground he grabbed my arm, or he would have gone down like a man who steps off a train in motion. He hung towards the bank of the road, feeling blindly, as it were, for the ground, with his free hand, as I eased him down. I got my blanket and calico from the pack saddle to make him comfortable.

"Help me with my back agen the tree," he said. "I must sit up—it's no use lyin' me down."

He sat with his hand gripping his side, and breathed painfully.

"Shall I run up to the hut and get the wife?" I asked.

"No." He spoke painfully. "No!" Then, as if the words were jerked out of him by a spasm: "She ain't there."

I took it that she had left him.

"How long have you been bad? How long has this been coming on?"

He took no notice of the question. I thought it was a touch of rheumatic fever, or something of that sort. "It's gone into my back and sides now—the pain's worse in me back," he said presently.

I had once been mates with a man who died suddenly of heart disease, while at work. He was washing a dish of dirt in the creek near a claim we were working; he let the dish slip into the water, fell back, crying, "O, my back!" and was gone. And now I felt by instinct that it was poor old Howlett's heart that was wrong. A man's heart is in his back as well as in his arms and hands.

The old man had turned pale with the pallor of a man who turns faint in a heat wave, and his arms fell loosely, and his hands rocked helplessly with the knuckles in the dust. I felt myself turning white, too, and the sick, cold, empty feeling in my stomach, for I knew the signs. Bushmen stand in awe of sickness and death.

But after I'd fixed him comfortably and given him a drink from the water bag the greyness left his face, and he pulled himself together a bit; he drew up his arms and folded them across his chest. He let his head rest back against the tree—his slouch hat had fallen off revealing a broad, white brow, much higher than I expected. He seemed to gaze on the azure fin of the range, showing above the dark blue-green bush on the horizon.

Then he commenced to speak—taking no notice of me when I asked him if he felt better now—to talk in that strange, absent, far-away tone that awes one. He told his story mechanically, monotonously—in set words, as I believe now, as he had often told it before; if not to others, then to the loneliness of the bush. And he used the names of people and places that I had never heard of—just as if I knew them as well as he did.

"I didn't want to bring her up the first year. It was no place for a woman. I wanted her to stay with her people and wait till I'd got the place a little more ship-shape. The Phippses took a selection down the creek. I wanted her to wait and come up with them so's she'd have some company—a woman to talk to. They came afterwards, but they didn't stop. It was no place for a woman.

"But Mary would come. She wouldn't stop with her people down country. She wanted to be with me, and look after me, and work and help me."

He repeated himself a great deal—said the same thing over and over again sometimes. He was only mad on one track. He'd tail off and sit silent for a while; then he'd become aware of me in a hurried, half-scared way, and apologise for putting me to all that trouble, and thank me. "I'll be all right d'reckly. Best take the horses up to the hut and have some breakfast; you'll find it by the fire. I'll foller you, d'reckly. The wife'll be waitin' an'—" He would drop off, and be going again presently on the old track:—

"Her mother was coming up to stay awhile at the end of the year, but the old man hurt his leg. Then her married sister was coming, but one of the youngsters got sick and there was trouble at home. I saw the doctor in the town—thirty miles from here—and fixed it up with him. He was a boozer—I'd 'a shot him afterwards. I fixed up with a woman in the town to come and stay. I thought Mary was wrong in her time. She must have been a month or six weeks out. But I listened to her.... Don't argue with a woman. Don't listen to a woman. Do the right thing. We should have had a mother woman to talk to us. But it was no place for a woman!"

He rocked his head, as if from some old agony of mind, against the tree-trunk.

"She was took bad suddenly one night, but it passed off. False alarm. I was going to ride somewhere, but she said to wait till daylight. Someone was sure to pass. She was a brave and sensible girl, but she had a terror of being left alone. It was no place for a woman!

"There was a black shepherd three or four miles away. I rode over while Mary was asleep, and started the black boy into town. I'd 'a shot him afterwards if I'd 'a caught him. The old black gin was dead the week before, or Mary would a' bin alright. She was tied up in a bunch with strips of blanket and greenhide, and put in a hole. So there wasn't even a gin near the place. It was no place for a woman!

"I was watchin' the road at daylight, and I was watchin' the road at dusk. I went down in the hollow and stooped down to get the gap agen the sky, so's I could see if anyone was comin' over.... I'd get on the horse and gallop along towards the town for five miles, but something would drag me back, and then I'd race for fear she'd die before I got to the hut. I expected the doctor every five minutes.

"It come on about daylight next morning. I ran back'ards and for'ards between the hut and the road like a madman. And no one come. I was running amongst the logs and stumps, and fallin' over them, when I saw a cloud of dust agen sunrise. It was her mother an' sister in the spring-cart, an' just catchin' up to them was the doctor in his buggy with the woman I'd arranged with in town. The mother and sister was staying at the town for the night, when they heard of the black boy. It took him a day to ride there. I'd 'a shot him if I'd 'a caught him ever after. The doctor'd been on the drunk. If I'd had the gun and known she was gone I'd have shot him in the buggy. They said she was dead. And the child was dead, too.

"They blamed me, but I didn't want her to come; it was no place for a woman. I never saw them again after the funeral. I didn't want to see them any more."

He moved his head wearily against the tree, and presently drifted on again in a softer tone—his eyes and voice were growing more absent and dreamy and far away.

"About a month after—or a year, I lost count of the time long ago—she came back to me. At first she'd come in the night, then sometimes when I was at work—and she had the baby—it was a girl—in her arms. And by-and-bye she came to stay altogether.... I didn't blame her for going away that time—it was no place for a woman.... She was a good wife to me. She was a jolly girl when I married her. The little girl grew up like her. I was going to send her down country to be educated—it was no place for a girl.

"But a month, or a year, ago, Mary left me, and took the daughter, and never came back till last night— this morning, I think it was. I thought at first it was the girl with her hair done up, and her mother's skirt on, to surprise her old dad. But it was Mary, my wife—as she was when I married her. She said she couldn't stay, but she'd wait for me on the road; on—the road...."

His arms fell, and his face went white. I got the water-bag. "Another turn like that and you'll be gone," I thought, as he came to again. Then I suddenly thought of a shanty that had been started, when I came that way last, ten or twelve miles along the road, towards the town. There was nothing for it but to leave him and ride on for help, and a cart of some kind.

"You wait here till I come back," I said. "I'm going for the doctor."

He roused himself a little. "Best come up to the hut and get some grub. The wife'll be waiting...." He was off the track again.

"Will you wait while I take the horse down to the creek?"

"Yes—I'll wait by the road."

"Look!" I said, "I'll leave the water-bag handy. Don't move till I come back."

"I won't move—I'll wait by the road," he said.

I took the packhorse, which was the freshest and best, threw the pack-saddle and bags into a bush, left the other horse to take care of itself, and started for the shanty, leaving the old man with his back to the tree, his arms folded, and his eyes on the horizon.

One of the chaps at the shanty rode on for the doctor at once, while the other came back with me in a spring-cart. He told me that old Howlett's wife had died in child-birth the first year on the selection— "she was a fine girl he'd heered!" He told me the story as the old man had told it, and in pretty well the same words, even to giving it as his opinion that it was no place for a woman. "And he 'hatted' and brooded over it till he went ratty."

I knew the rest. He not only thought that his wife, or the ghost of his wife, had been with him all those years, but that the child had lived and grown up, and that the wife did the housework; which, of course, he must have done himself.

When we reached him his knotted hands had fallen for the last time, and they were at rest. I only took one quick look at his face, but could have sworn that he was gazing at the blue fin of the range on the horizon of the bush.

Up at the hut the table was set as on the first day I saw it, and breakfast in the camp-oven by the fire.

Mitchell's Jobs

"I'm going to knock off work and try to make some money," said Mitchell, as he jerked the tea-leaves out of his pannikin and reached for the billy. "It's been the great mistake of my life—if I hadn't wasted all my time and energy working and looking for work I might have been an independent man to-day."

"Joe!" he added in a louder voice, condescendingly adapting his language to my bushed comprehension. "I'm going to sling graft and try and get some stuff together."

I didn't feel in a responsive humour, but I lit up and settled back comfortably against the tree, and Jack folded his arms on his knees and presently continued, reflectively:

"I remember the first time I went to work. I was a youngster then. Mother used to go round looking for jobs for me. She reckoned, perhaps, that I was too shy to go in where there was a boy wanted and barrack for myself properly, and she used to help me and see me through to the best of her ability. I'm afraid I didn't always feel as grateful to her as I should have felt. I was a thankless kid at the best of times—most kids are—but otherwise I was a straight enough little chap as nippers go. Sometimes I almost wish I hadn't been. My relations would have thought a good deal more of me and treated me better—and, besides, it's a comfort, at times, to sit and watch the sun going down in the bed of the bush, and think of your wicked childhood and wasted life, and the way you treated your parents and broke their hearts, and feel just properly repentant and bitter and remorseful and low-spirited about it when it's too late.

"Ah, well!... I generally did feel a bit backward in going in when I came to the door of an office or shop where there was a 'Strong Lad', or a 'Willing Youth', wanted inside to make himself generally useful. I was a strong lad and a willing youth enough, in some things, for that matter; but I didn't like to see it written up on a card in a shop window, and I didn't want to make myself generally useful in a close shop in a hot dusty street on mornings when the weather was fine and the great sunny rollers were coming in grand on the Bondi Beach and down at Coogee, and I could swim.... I'd give something to be down along there now."

Mitchell looked away out over the sultry sandy plain that we were to tackle next day, and sighed.

"The first job I got was in a jam factory. They only had 'Boy Wanted' on the card in the window, and I thought it would suit me. They set me to work to peel peaches, and, as soon as the foreman's back was turned, I picked out a likely-looking peach and tried it. They soaked those peaches in salt or acid or something—it was part of the process—and I had to spit it out. Then I got an orange from a boy who was slicing them, but it was bitter, and I couldn't eat it. I saw that I'd been had properly. I was in a fix, and had to get out of it the best way I could. I'd left my coat down in the front shop, and the foreman and boss were there, so I had to work in that place for two mortal hours. It was about the longest two hours I'd ever spent in my life. At last the foreman came up, and I told him I wanted to go down to the back for a minute. I slipped down, watched my chance till the boss' back was turned, got my coat, and cleared.

"The next job I got was in a mat factory; at least, Aunt got that for me. I didn't want to have anything to do with mats or carpets. The worst of it was the boss didn't seem to want me to go, and I had a job to get him to sack me, and when he did he saw some of my people and took me back again next week. He sacked me finally the next Saturday.

"I got the next job myself. I didn't hurry; I took my time and picked out a good one. It was in a lolly factory. I thought it would suit me—and it did, for a while. They put me on stirring up and mixing stuff in the jujube department; but I got so sick of the smell of it and so full of jujube and other lollies that I soon wanted a change; so I had a row with the chief of the jujube department and the boss gave me the sack.

"I got a job in a grocery then. I thought I'd have more variety there. But one day the boss was away, sick or something, all the afternoon, and I sold a lot of things too cheap. I didn't know. When a customer came in and asked for something I'd just look round in the window till I saw a card with the price written up on it, and sell the best quality according to that price; and once or twice I made a mistake the other way about and lost a couple of good customers. It was a hot, drowsy afternoon, and by-and-bye I began to feel dull and sleepy. So I looked round the corner and saw a Chinaman coming. I got a big tin garden syringe and filled it full of brine from the butter keg, and, when he came opposite the door, I let him have the full force of it in the ear.

"That Chinaman put down his baskets and came for me. I was strong for my age, and thought I could fight, but he gave me a proper mauling.

"It was like running up against a thrashing machine, and it wouldn't have been well for me if the boss of the shop next door hadn't interfered. He told my boss, and my boss gave me the sack at once.

"I took a spell of eighteen months or so after that, and was growing up happy and contented when a married sister of mine must needs come to live in town and interfere. I didn't like married sisters, though I always got on grand with my brothers-in-law, and wished there were more of them. The married sister comes round and cleans up the place and pulls your things about and finds your pipe and tobacco and things, and cigarette portraits, and "Deadwood Dicks", that you've got put away all right, so's your mother and aunt wouldn't find them in a generation of cats, and says:

"'Mother, why don't you make that boy go to work. It's a scandalous shame to see a big boy like that growing up idle. He's going to the bad before your eyes.' And she's always trying to make out that you're a liar, and trying to make mother believe it, too. My married sister got me a job with a chemist, whose missus she knew.

"I got on pretty well there, and by-and-bye I was put upstairs in the grinding and mixing department; but, after a while, they put another boy that I was chummy with up there with me, and that was a mistake. I didn't think so at the time, but I can see it now. We got up to all sorts of tricks. We'd get mixing together chemicals that weren't related to see how they'd agree, and we nearly blew up the shop several times, and set it on fire once. But all the chaps liked us, and fixed things up for us. One day we got a big black dog—that we meant to take home that evening—and sneaked him upstairs and put him on a flat roof outside the laboratory. He had a touch of the mange and didn't look well, so we gave him a dose of something; and he scrambled over the parapet and slipped down a steep iron roof in front, and fell on a respected townsman that knew my people. We were awfully frightened, and didn't say anything. Nobody saw it but us. The dog had the presence of mind to leave at once, and the respected townsman was picked up and taken home in a cab; and he got it hot from his wife, too, I believe, for being in that drunken, beastly state in the main street in the middle of the day.

"I don't think he was ever quite sure that he hadn't been drunk or what had happened, for he had had one or two that morning; so it didn't matter much. Only we lost the dog.

"One day I went downstairs to the packing-room and saw a lot of phosphorus in jars of water. I wanted to fix up a ghost for Billy, my mate, so I nicked a bit and slipped it into my trouser pocket.

"I stood under the tap and let it pour on me. The phosphorus burnt clean through my pocket and fell on the ground. I was sent home that night with my leg dressed with lime-water and oil, and a pair of the boss's pants on that were about half a yard too long for me, and I felt miserable enough, too. They said it would stop my tricks for a while, and so it did. I'll carry the mark to my dying day—and for two or three days after, for that matter."

I fell asleep at this point, and left Mitchell's cattle pup to hear it out.

Bill, the Ventriloquial Rooster

"When we were up country on the selection, we had a rooster at our place, named Bill," said Mitchell; "a big mongrel of no particular breed, though the old lady said he was a 'brammer'—and many an argument she had with the old man about it too; she was just as stubborn and obstinate in her opinion as the governor was in his. But, anyway, we called him Bill, and didn't take any particular notice of him till a cousin of some of us came from Sydney on a visit to the country, and stayed at our place because it was cheaper than stopping at a pub. Well, somehow this chap got interested in Bill, and studied him for two or three days, and at last he says:

"'Why, that rooster's a ventriloquist!'

"'A what?'

"'A ventriloquist!'

"'Go along with yer!'

"'But he is. I've heard of cases like this before; but this is the first I've come across. Bill's a ventriloquist right enough.'

"Then we remembered that there wasn't another rooster within five miles—our only neighbour, an Irishman named Page, didn't have one at the time—and we'd often heard another cock crow, but didn't think to take any notice of it. We watched Bill, and sure enough he WAS a ventriloquist. The 'ka-cocka' would come all right, but the 'co-ka-koo-oi-oo' seemed to come from a distance. And sometimes the whole crow would go wrong, and come back like an echo that had been lost for a year. Bill would stand on tiptoe, and hold his elbows out, and curve his neck, and go two or three times as if he was swallowing nest-eggs, and nearly break his neck and burst his gizzard; and then there'd be no sound at all where he was—only a cock crowing in the distance.

"And pretty soon we could see that Bill was in great trouble about it himself. You see, he didn't know it was himself—thought it was another rooster challenging him, and he wanted badly to find that other bird. He would get up on the wood-heap, and crow and listen—crow and listen again—crow and listen, and then he'd go up to the top of the paddock, and get up on the stack, and crow and listen there. Then down to the other end of the paddock, and get up on a mullock-heap, and crow and listen there. Then across to the other side and up on a log among the saplings, and crow 'n' listen some more. He searched all over the place for that other rooster, but, of course, couldn't find him. Sometimes he'd be out all day crowing and listening all over the country, and then come home dead tired, and rest and cool off in a hole that the hens had scratched for him in a damp place under the water-cask sledge.

"Well, one day Page brought home a big white rooster, and when he let it go it climbed up on Page's stack and crowed, to see if there was any more roosters round there. Bill had come home tired; it was a hot day, and he'd rooted out the hens, and was having a spell-oh under the cask when the white rooster crowed. Bill didn't lose any time getting out and on to the wood-heap, and then he waited till he heard the crow again; then he crowed, and the other rooster crowed again, and they crowed at each other for three days, and called each other all the wretches they could lay their tongues to, and after that they implored each other to come out and be made into chicken soup and feather pillows. But neither'd come. You see, there were THREE crows—there was Bill's crow, and the ventriloquist crow, and the white rooster's crow—and each rooster thought that there was TWO roosters in the opposition camp, and that he mightn't get fair play, and, consequently, both were afraid to put up their hands.

"But at last Bill couldn't stand it any longer. He made up his mind to go and have it out, even if there was a whole agricultural show of prize and honourable-mention fighting-cocks in Page's yard. He got down from the wood-heap and started off across the ploughed field, his head down, his elbows out, and his thick awkward legs prodding away at the furrows behind for all they were worth.

"I wanted to go down badly and see the fight, and barrack for Bill. But I daren't, because I'd been coming up the road late the night before with my brother Joe, and there was about three panels of turkeys roosting along on the top rail of Page's front fence; and we brushed 'em with a bough, and they got up such a blessed gobbling fuss about it that Page came out in his shirt and saw us running away; and I knew he was laying for us with a bullock whip. Besides, there was friction between the two families on account of a thoroughbred bull that Page borrowed and wouldn't lend to us, and that got into our paddock on account of me mending a panel in the party fence, and carelessly leaving the top rail down after sundown while our cows was moving round there in the saplings.

"So there was too much friction for me to go down, but I climbed a tree as near the fence as I could and watched. Bill reckoned he'd found that rooster at last. The white rooster wouldn't come down from the stack, so Bill went up to him, and they fought there till they tumbled down the other side, and I couldn't see any more. Wasn't I wild? I'd have given my dog to have seen the rest of the fight. I went down to the far side of Page's fence and climbed a tree there, but, of course, I couldn't see anything, so I came home the back way. Just as I got home Page came round to the front and sung out, 'Insoid there!' And me and Jim went under the house like snakes and looked out round a pile. But Page was all right—he had a broad grin on his face, and Bill safe under his arm. He put Bill down on the ground very carefully, and says he to the old folks:

"'Yer rooster knocked the stuffin' out of my rooster, but I bear no malice. 'Twas a grand foight.'

"And then the old man and Page had a yarn, and got pretty friendly after that. And Bill didn't seem to bother about any more ventriloquism; but the white rooster spent a lot of time looking for that other rooster. Perhaps he thought he'd have better luck with him. But Page was on the look-out all the time to get a rooster that would lick ours. He did nothing else for a month but ride round and enquire about roosters; and at last he borrowed a game-bird in town, left five pounds deposit on him, and brought him home. And Page and the old man agreed to have a match—about the only thing they'd agreed about for five years. And they fixed it up for a Sunday when the old lady and the girls and kids were going on a visit to some relations, about fifteen miles away—to stop all night. The guv'nor made me go with them on horseback; but I knew what was up, and so my pony went lame about a mile along the road, and I had to come back and turn him out in the top paddock, and hide the saddle and bridle in a hollow log, and sneak home and climb up on the roof of the shed. It was a awful hot day, and I had to keep climbing backward and forward over the ridge-pole all the morning to keep out of sight of the old man, for he was moving about a good deal.

"Well, after dinner, the fellows from roundabout began to ride in and hang up their horses round the place till it looked as if there was going to be a funeral. Some of the chaps saw me, of course, but I tipped them the wink, and they gave me the office whenever the old man happened around.

"Well, Page came along with his game-rooster. Its name was Jim. It wasn't much to look at, and it seemed a good deal smaller and weaker than Bill. Some of the chaps were disgusted, and said it wasn't a game-rooster at all; Bill'd settle it in one lick, and they wouldn't have any fun.

"Well, they brought the game one out and put him down near the wood-heap, and rousted Bill out from under his cask. He got interested at once. He looked at Jim, and got up on the wood-heap and crowed and looked at Jim again. He reckoned THIS at last was the fowl that had been humbugging him all along. Presently his trouble caught him, and then he'd crow and take a squint at the game 'un, and crow again, and have another squint at gamey, and try to crow and keep his eye on the game-rooster at the same time. But Jim never committed himself, until at last he happened to gape just after Bill's whole crow went wrong, and Bill spotted him. He reckoned he'd caught him this time, and he got down off that wood-heap and went for the foe. But Jim ran away—and Bill ran after him.

"Round and round the wood-heap they went, and round the shed, and round the house and under it, and back again, and round the wood-heap and over it and round the other way, and kept it up for close on an hour. Bill's bill was just within an inch or so of the game-rooster's tail feathers most of the time, but he couldn't get any nearer, do how he liked. And all the time the fellers kept chyackin Page and singing out, 'What price yer game 'un, Page! Go it, Bill! Go it, old cock!' and all that sort of thing. Well, the game-rooster went as if it was a go-as-you-please, and he didn't care if it lasted a year. He didn't seem to take any interest in the business, but Bill got excited, and by-and-by he got mad. He held his head lower and lower and his wings further and further out from his sides, and prodded away harder and harder at the ground behind, but it wasn't any use. Jim seemed to keep ahead without trying. They stuck to the wood-heap towards the last. They went round first one way for a while, and then the other for a change, and now and then they'd go over the top to break the monotony; and the chaps got more interested in the race than they would have been in the fight—and bet on it, too. But Bill was handicapped with his weight. He was done up at last; he slowed down till he couldn't waddle, and then, when he was thoroughly knocked up, that game-rooster turned on him, and gave him the father of a hiding.

"And my father caught me when I'd got down in the excitement, and wasn't thinking, and HE gave ME the step-father of a hiding. But he had a lively time with the old lady afterwards, over the cock-fight.

"Bill was so disgusted with himself that he went under the cask and died."

Bush Cats

"Domestic cats" we mean—the descendants of cats who came from the northern world during the last hundred odd years. We do not know the name of the vessel in which the first Thomas and his Maria came out to Australia, but we suppose that it was one of the ships of the First Fleet. Most likely Maria had kittens on the voyage—two lots, perhaps—the majority of which were buried at sea; and no doubt the disembarkation caused her much maternal anxiety.

The feline race has not altered much in Australia, from a physical point of view—not yet. The rabbit has developed into something like a cross between a kangaroo and a possum, but the bush has not begun to develop the common cat. She is just as sedate and motherly as the mummy cats of Egypt were, but she takes longer strolls of nights, climbs gum-trees instead of roofs, and hunts stranger vermin than ever came under the observation of her northern ancestors. Her views have widened. She is mostly thinner than the English farm cat—which is, they say, on account of eating lizards.

English rats and English mice—we say "English" because everything which isn't Australian in Australia, IS English (or British)—English rats and English mice are either rare or non-existent in the bush; but the hut cat has a wider range for game. She is always dragging in things which are unknown in the halls of zoology; ugly, loathsome, crawling abortions which have not been classified yet—and perhaps could not be.

The Australian zoologist ought to rake up some more dead languages, and then go Out Back with a few bush cats.

The Australian bush cat has a nasty, unpleasant habit of dragging a long, wriggling, horrid, black snake—she seems to prefer black snakes—into a room where there are ladies, proudly laying it down in a conspicuous place (usually in front of the exit), and then looking up for approbation. She wonders, perhaps, why the visitors are in such a hurry to leave.

Pussy doesn't approve of live snakes round the place, especially if she has kittens; and if she finds a snake in the vicinity of her progeny—well, it is bad for that particular serpent.

This brings recollections of a neighbour's cat who went out in the scrub, one midsummer's day, and found a brown snake. Her name—the cat's name—was Mary Ann. She got hold of the snake all right, just within an inch of its head; but it got the rest of its length wound round her body and squeezed about eight lives out of her. She had the presence of mind to keep her hold; but it struck her that she was in a fix, and that if she wanted to save her ninth life, it wouldn't be a bad idea to go home for help. So she started home, snake and all.

The family were at dinner when Mary Ann came in, and, although she stood on an open part of the floor, no one noticed her for a while. She couldn't ask for help, for her mouth was too full of snake. By-and-bye one of the girls glanced round, and then went over the table, with a shriek, and out of the back door. The room was cleared very quickly. The eldest boy got a long-handled shovel, and in another second would have killed more cat than snake; but his father interfered. The father was a shearer, and Mary Ann was a favourite cat with him. He got a pair of shears from the shelf and deftly shore off the snake's head, and one side of Mary Ann's whiskers. She didn't think it safe to let go yet. She kept her teeth in the neck until the selector snipped the rest of the snake off her. The bits were carried out on a shovel to die at sundown. Mary Ann had a good drink of milk, and then got her tongue out and licked herself back into the proper shape for a cat; after which she went out to look for that snake's mate. She found it, too, and dragged it home the same evening.

Cats will kill rabbits and drag them home. We knew a fossicker whose cat used to bring him a bunny nearly every night. The fossicker had rabbits for breakfast until he got sick of them, and then he used to swap them with a butcher for meat. The cat was named Ingersoll, which indicates his sex and gives an inkling to his master's religious and political opinions. Ingersoll used to prospect round in the gloaming until he found some rabbit holes which showed encouraging indications. He would shepherd one hole for an hour or so every evening until he found it was a duffer, or worked it out; then he would shift to another. One day he prospected a big hollow log with a lot of holes in it, and more going down underneath. The indications were very good, but Ingersoll had no luck. The game had too many ways of getting out and in. He found that he could not work that claim by himself, so he floated it into a company. He persuaded several cats from a neighbouring selection to take shares, and they watched the holes together, or in turns—they worked shifts. The dividends more than realised even their wildest expectations, for each cat took home at least one rabbit every night for a week.

A selector started a vegetable garden about the time when rabbits were beginning to get troublesome up country. The hare had not shown itself yet. The farmer kept quite a regiment of cats to protect his garden—and they protected it. He would shut the cats up all day with nothing to eat, and let them out about sundown; then they would mooch off to the turnip patch like farm-labourers going to work. They would drag the rabbits home to the back door, and sit there and watch them until the farmer opened the door and served out the ration of milk. Then the cats would turn in. He nearly always found a semi-circle of dead rabbits and watchful cats round the door in the morning. They sold the product of their labour direct to the farmer for milk. It didn't matter if one cat had been unlucky—had not got a rabbit—each had an equal share in the general result. They were true socialists, those cats.

One of those cats was a mighty big Tom, named Jack. He was death on rabbits; he would work hard all night, laying for them and dragging them home. Some weeks he would graft every night, and at other times every other night, but he was generally pretty regular. When he reckoned he had done an extra night's work, he would take the next night off and go three miles to the nearest neighbour's to see his Maria and take her out for a stroll. Well, one evening Jack went into the garden and chose a place where there was good cover, and lay low. He was a bit earlier than usual, so he thought he would have a doze till rabbit time. By-and-bye he heard a noise, and slowly, cautiously opening one eye, he saw two big ears sticking out of the leaves in front of him. He judged that it was an extra big bunny, so he put some extra style into his manoeuvres. In about five minutes he made his spring. He must have thought (if cats think) that it was a whopping, old-man rabbit, for it was a pioneer hare—not an ordinary English hare, but one of those great coarse, lanky things which the bush is breeding. The selector was attracted by an unusual commotion and a cloud of dust among his cabbages, and came along with his gun in time to witness the fight. First Jack would drag the hare, and then the hare would drag Jack; sometimes they would be down together, and then Jack would use his hind claws with effect; finally he got his teeth in the right place, and triumphed. Then he started to drag the corpse home, but he had to give it best and ask his master to lend a hand. The selector took up the hare, and Jack followed home, much to the family's surprise. He did not go back to work that night; he took a spell. He had a drink of milk, licked the dust off himself, washed it down with another drink, and sat in front of the fire and thought for a goodish while. Then he got up, walked over to the corner where the hare was lying, had a good look at it, came back to the fire, sat down again, and thought hard. He was still thinking when the family retired.

Meeting Old Mates

I

Tom Smith

You are getting well on in the thirties, and haven't left off being a fool yet. You have been away in another colony or country for a year or so, and have now come back again. Most of your chums have gone away or got married, or, worse still, signed the pledge—settled down and got steady; and you feel lonely and desolate and left-behind enough for anything. While drifting aimlessly round town with an eye out for some chance acquaintance to have a knock round with, you run against an old chum whom you never dreamt of meeting, or whom you thought to be in some other part of the country—or perhaps you knock up against someone who knows the old chum in question, and he says:

"I suppose you know Tom Smith's in Sydney?"

"Tom Smith! Why, I thought he was in Queensland! I haven't seen him for more than three years. Where's the old joker hanging out at all? Why, except you, there's no one in Australia I'd sooner see than Tom Smith. Here I've been mooning round like an unemployed for three weeks, looking for someone to have a knock round with, and Tom in Sydney all the time. I wish I'd known before. Where'll I run against him—where does he live?"

"Oh, he's living at home."

"But where's his home? I was never there."

"Oh, I'll give you his address.... There, I think that's it. I'm not sure about the number, but you'll soon find out in that street—most of 'em'll know Tom Smith."

"Thanks! I rather think they will. I'm glad I met you. I'll hunt Tom up to-day."

So you put a few shillings in your pocket, tell your landlady that you're going to visit an old aunt of yours or a sick friend, and mayn't be home that night; and then you start out to hunt up Tom Smith and have at least one more good night, if you die for it.

This is the first time you have seen Tom at home; you knew of his home and people in the old days, but only in a vague, indefinite sort of way. Tom has changed! He is stouter and older-looking; he seems solemn and settled down. You intended to give him a surprise and have a good old jolly laugh with him, but somehow things get suddenly damped at the beginning. He grins and grips your hand right enough, but there seems something wanting. You can't help staring at him, and he seems to look at you in a strange, disappointing way; it doesn't strike you that you also have changed, and perhaps more in his eyes than he in yours. He introduces you to his mother and sisters and brothers, and the rest of the family; or to his wife, as the case may be; and you have to suppress your feelings and be polite and talk common-place. You hate to be polite and talk common-place. You aren't built that way—and Tom wasn't either, in the old days. The wife (or the mother and sisters) receives you kindly, for Tom's sake, and makes much of you; but they don't know you yet. You want to get Tom outside, and have a yarn and a drink and a laugh with him—you are bursting to tell him all about yourself, and get him to tell you all about himself, and ask him if he remembers things; and you wonder if he is bursting the same way, and hope he is. The old lady and sisters (or the wife) bore you pretty soon, and you wonder if they bore Tom; you almost fancy, from his looks, that they do. You wonder whether Tom is coming out to-night, whether he wants to get out, and if he wants to and wants to get out by himself, whether he'll be able to manage it; but you daren't broach the subject, it wouldn't be polite. You've got to be polite. Then you get worried by the thought that Tom is bursting to get out with you and only wants an excuse; is waiting, in fact, and hoping for you to ask him in an off-hand sort of way to come out for a stroll. But you're not quite sure; and besides, if you were, you wouldn't have the courage. By-and-bye you get tired of it all, thirsty, and want to get out in the open air. You get tired of saying, "Do you really, Mrs. Smith?" or "Do you think so, Miss Smith?" or "You were quite right, Mrs. Smith," and "Well, I think so too, Mrs. Smith," or, to the brother, "That's just what I thought, Mr. Smith." You don't want to "talk pretty" to them, and listen to their wishy-washy nonsense; you want to get out and have a roaring spree with Tom, as you had in the old days; you want to make another night of it with your old mate, Tom Smith; and pretty soon you get the blues badly, and feel nearly smothered in there, and you've got to get out and have a beer anyway—Tom or no Tom; and you begin to feel wild with Tom himself; and at last you make a bold dash for it and chance Tom. You get up, look at your hat, and say: "Ah, well, I must be going, Tom; I've got to meet someone down the street at seven o'clock. Where'll I meet you in town next week?"

But Tom says:

"Oh, dash it; you ain't going yet. Stay to tea, Joe, stay to tea. It'll be on the table in a minute. Sit down—sit down, man! Here, gimme your hat."

And Tom's sister, or wife, or mother comes in with an apron on and her hands all over flour, and says:

"Oh, you're not going yet, Mr. Brown? Tea'll be ready in a minute. Do stay for tea." And if you make excuses, she cross-examines you about the time you've got to keep that appointment down the street, and tells you that their clock is twenty minutes fast, and that you have got plenty of time, and so you have to give in. But you are mightily encouraged by a winksome expression which you see, or fancy you see, on your side of Tom's face; also by the fact of his having accidentally knocked his foot against your shins. So you stay.

One of the females tells you to "Sit there, Mr. Brown," and you take your place at the table, and the polite business goes on. You've got to hold your knife and fork properly, and mind your p's and q's, and when she says, "Do you take milk and sugar, Mr. Brown?" you've got to say, "Yes, please, Miss Smith—thanks—that's plenty." And when they press you, as they will, to have more, you've got to keep on saying, "No, thanks, Mrs. Smith; no, thanks, Miss Smith; I really couldn't; I've done very well, thank you; I had a very late dinner, and so on"—bother such tommy-rot. And you don't seem to have any appetite, anyway. And you think of the days out on the track when you and Tom sat on your swags under a mulga at mid-day, and ate mutton and johnny-cake with clasp-knives, and drank by turns out of the old, battered, leaky billy.

And after tea you have to sit still while the precious minutes are wasted, and listen and sympathize, while all the time you are on the fidget to get out with Tom, and go down to a private bar where you know some girls.

And perhaps by-and-bye the old lady gets confidential, and seizes an opportunity to tell you what a good steady young fellow Tom is now that he never touches drink, and belongs to a temperance society (or the Y.M.C.A.), and never stays out of nights.

Consequently you feel worse than ever, and lonelier, and sorrier that you wasted your time coming. You are encouraged again by a glimpse of Tom putting on a clean collar and fixing himself up a bit; but when you are ready to go, and ask him if he's coming a bit down the street with you, he says he thinks he will in such a disinterested, don't-mind-if-I-do sort of tone, that he makes you mad.

At last, after promising to "drop in again, Mr. Brown, whenever you're passing," and to "don't forget to call," and thanking them for their assurance that they'll "be always glad to see you," and telling them that you've spent a very pleasant evening and enjoyed yourself, and are awfully sorry you couldn't stay—you get away with Tom.

You don't say much to each other till you get round the corner and down the street a bit, and then for a while your conversation is mostly common-place, such as, "Well, how have you been getting on all this time, Tom?" "Oh, all right. How have you been getting on?" and so on.

But presently, and perhaps just as you have made up your mind to chance the alleged temperance business and ask Tom in to have a drink, he throws a glance up and down the street, nudges your shoulder, says "Come on," and disappears sideways into a pub.

"What's yours, Tom?" "What's yours, Joe?" "The same for me." "Well, here's luck, old man." "Here's luck." You take a drink, and look over your glass at Tom. Then the old smile spreads over his face, and it makes you glad—you could swear to Tom's grin in a hundred years. Then something tickles him—your expression, perhaps, or a recollection of the past—and he sets down his glass on the bar and laughs. Then you laugh. Oh, there's no smile like the smile that old mates favour each other with over the tops of their glasses when they meet again after years. It is eloquent, because of the memories that give it birth.

"Here's another. Do you remember—? Do you remember—?" Oh, it all comes back again like a flash. Tom hasn't changed a bit; just the same good-hearted, jolly idiot he always was. Old times back again! "It's just like old times," says Tom, after three or four more drinks.

And so you make a night of it and get uproariously jolly. You get as "glorious" as Bobby Burns did in the part of Tam O'Shanter, and have a better "time" than any of the times you had in the old days. And you see Tom as nearly home in the morning as you dare, and he reckons he'll get it hot from his people—which no doubt he will—and he explains that they are very particular up at home—church people, you know—and, of course, especially if he's married, it's understood between you that you'd better not call for him up at home after this—at least, not till things have cooled down a bit. It's always the way. The friend of the husband always gets the blame in cases like this. But Tom fixes up a yarn to tell them, and you aren't to "say anything different" in case you run against any of them. And he fixes up an appointment with you for next Saturday night, and he'll get there if he gets divorced for it. But he MIGHT have to take the wife out shopping, or one of the girls somewhere; and if you see her with him you've got to lay low, and be careful, and wait—at another hour and place, perhaps, all of which is arranged—for if she sees you she'll smell a rat at once, and he won't be able to get off at all.

And so, as far as you and Tom are concerned, the "old times" have come back once more.

But, of course (and we almost forgot it), you might chance to fall in love with one of Tom's sisters, in which case there would be another and a totally different story to tell.

II

Jack Ellis

Things are going well with you. You have escaped from "the track", so to speak, and are in a snug, comfortable little billet in the city. Well, while doing the block you run against an old mate of other days—VERY other days—call him Jack Ellis. Things have gone hard with Jack. He knows you at once, but makes no advance towards a greeting; he acts as though he thinks you might cut him—which, of course, if you are a true mate, you have not the slightest intention of doing. His coat is yellow and frayed, his hat is battered and green, his trousers "gone" in various places, his linen very cloudy, and his boots burst and innocent of polish. You try not to notice these things—or rather, not to seem to notice them—but you cannot help doing so, and you are afraid he'll notice that you see these things, and put a wrong construction on it. How men will misunderstand each other! You greet him with more than the necessary enthusiasm. In your anxiety to set him at his ease and make him believe that nothing—not even money—can make a difference in your friendship, you over-act the business; and presently you are afraid that he'll notice that too, and put a wrong construction on it. You wish that your collar was not so clean, nor your clothes so new. Had you known you would meet him, you would have put on some old clothes for the occasion.

You are both embarrassed, but it is YOU who feel ashamed—you are almost afraid to look at him lest he'll think you are looking at his shabbiness. You ask him in to have a drink, but he doesn't respond so heartily as you wish, as he did in the old days; he doesn't like drinking with anybody when he isn't "fixed", as he calls it—when he can't shout.

It didn't matter in the old days who held the money so long as there was plenty of "stuff" in the camp. You think of the days when Jack stuck to you through thick and thin. You would like to give him money now, but he is so proud; he always was; he makes you mad with his beastly pride. There wasn't any pride of that sort on the track or in the camp in those days; but times have changed—your lives have drifted too widely apart—you have taken different tracks since then; and Jack, without intending to, makes you feel that it is so.

You have a drink, but it isn't a success; it falls flat, as far as Jack is concerned; he won't have another; he doesn't "feel on", and presently he escapes under plea of an engagement, and promises to see you again.

And you wish that the time was come when no one could have more or less to spend than another.

P.S.—I met an old mate of that description once, and so successfully persuaded him out of his beastly pride that he borrowed two pounds off me till Monday. I never got it back since, and I want it badly at the present time. In future I'll leave old mates with their pride unimpaired.

Two Larrikins

"Y'orter do something, Ernie. Yer know how I am. YOU don't seem to care. Y'orter to do something."

Stowsher slouched at a greater angle to the greasy door-post, and scowled under his hat-brim. It was a little, low, frowsy room opening into Jones' Alley. She sat at the table, sewing—a thin, sallow girl with weak, colourless eyes. She looked as frowsy as her surroundings.

"Well, why don't you go to some of them women, and get fixed up?"

She flicked the end of the table-cloth over some tiny, unfinished articles of clothing, and bent to her work.

"But you know very well I haven't got a shilling, Ernie," she said, quietly. "Where am I to get the money from?"

"Who asked yer to get it?"

She was silent, with the exasperating silence of a woman who has determined to do a thing in spite of all reasons and arguments that may be brought against it.

"Well, wot more do yer want?" demanded Stowsher, impatiently.

She bent lower. "Couldn't we keep it, Ernie?"

"Wot next?" asked Stowsher, sulkily—he had half suspected what was coming. Then, with an impatient oath, "You must be gettin' ratty."

She brushed the corner of the cloth further over the little clothes.

"It wouldn't cost anything, Ernie. I'd take a pride in him, and keep him clean, and dress him like a little lord. He'll be different from all the other youngsters. He wouldn't be like those dirty, sickly little brats out there. He'd be just like you, Ernie; I know he would. I'll look after him night and day, and bring him up well and strong. We'd train his little muscles from the first, Ernie, and he'd be able to knock 'em all out when he grew up. It wouldn't cost much, and I'd work hard and be careful if you'd help me. And you'd be proud of him, too, Ernie—I know you would."

Stowsher scraped the doorstep with his foot; but whether he was "touched", or feared hysterics and was wisely silent, was not apparent.

"Do you remember the first day I met you, Ernie?" she asked, presently.

Stowsher regarded her with an uneasy scowl: "Well—wot o' that?"

"You came into the bar-parlour at the 'Cricketers' Arms' and caught a push of 'em chyacking your old man."

"Well, I altered that."

"I know you did. You done for three of them, one after another, and two was bigger than you."

"Yes! and when the push come up we done for the rest," said Stowsher, softening at the recollection.

"And the day you come home and caught the landlord bullying your old mother like a dog—"

"Yes; I got three months for that job. But it was worth it!" he reflected. "Only," he added, "the old woman might have had the knocker to keep away from the lush while I was in quod.... But wot's all this got to do with it?"

"HE might barrack and fight for you, some day, Ernie," she said softly, "when you're old and out of form and ain't got no push to back you."

The thing was becoming decidedly embarrassing to Stowsher; not that he felt any delicacy on the subject, but because he hated to be drawn into a conversation that might be considered "soft".

"Oh, stow that!" he said, comfortingly. "Git on yer hat, and I'll take yer for a trot."

She rose quickly, but restrained herself, recollecting that it was not good policy to betray eagerness in response to an invitation from Ernie.

"But—you know—I don't like to go out like this. You can't—you wouldn't like to take me out the way I am, Ernie!"

"Why not? Wot rot!"

"The fellows would see me, and—and—"

"And... wot?"

"They might notice—"

"Well, wot o' that? I want 'em to. Are yer comin' or are yer ain't? Fling round now. I can't hang on here all day."

They walked towards Flagstaff Hill.

One or two, slouching round a pub. corner, saluted with "Wotcher, Stowsher!"

"Not too stinkin'," replied Stowsher. "Soak yer heads."

"Stowsher's goin' to stick," said one privately.

"An' so he orter," said another. "Wish I had the chanst."

The two turned up a steep lane.

"Don't walk so fast up hill, Ernie; I can't, you know."

"All right, Liz. I forgot that. Why didn't yer say so before?"

She was contentedly silent most of the way, warned by instinct, after the manner of women when they have gained their point by words.

Once he glanced over his shoulder with a short laugh. "Gorblime!" he said, "I nearly thought the little beggar was a-follerin' along behind!"

When he left her at the door he said: "Look here, Liz. 'Ere's half a quid. Git what yer want. Let her go. I'm goin' to graft again in the mornin', and I'll come round and see yer to-morrer night."

Still she seemed troubled and uneasy.

"Ernie."

"Well. Wot now?"

"S'posin' it's a girl, Ernie."

Stowsher flung himself round impatiently.

"Oh, for God's sake, stow that! Yer always singin' out before yer hurt.... There's somethin' else, ain't there—while the bloomin' shop's open?"

"No, Ernie. Ain't you going to kiss me?... I'm satisfied."

"Satisfied! Yer don't want the kid to be arst 'oo 'is father was, do yer? Yer'd better come along with me some day this week and git spliced. Yer don't want to go frettin' or any of that funny business while it's on."

"Oh, Ernie! do you really mean it?"—and she threw her arms round his neck, and broke down at last.

"So-long, Liz. No more funny business now—I've had enough of it. Keep yer pecker up, old girl. To-morrer night, mind." Then he added suddenly: "Yer might have known I ain't that sort of a bloke"—and left abruptly.

Liz was very happy.

Mr. Smellingscheck

I met him in a sixpenny restaurant—"All meals, 6d.—Good beds, 1s." That was before sixpenny restaurants rose to a third-class position, and became possibly respectable places to live in, through the establishment, beneath them, of fourpenny hash-houses (good beds, 6d.), and, beneath THEM again, of THREE-penny "dining-rooms—CLEAN beds, 4d."

There were five beds in our apartment, the head of one against the foot of the next, and so on round the room, with a space where the door and washstand were. I chose the bed the head of which was near the foot of his, because he looked like a man who took his bath regularly. I should like, in the interests of sentiment, to describe the place as a miserable, filthy, evil-smelling garret; but I can't—because it wasn't. The room was large and airy; the floor was scrubbed and the windows cleaned at least once a week, and the beds kept fresh and neat, which is more—a good deal more—than can be said of many genteel private boarding-houses. The lodgers were mostly respectable unemployed, and one or two—fortunate men!—in work; it was the casual boozer, the professional loafer, and the occasional spieler—the one-shilling-bed-men—who made the place objectionable, not the hard-working people who paid ten pounds a week for the house; and, but for the one-night lodgers and the big gilt black-and-red bordered and "shaded" "6d." in the window—which made me glance guiltily up and down the street, like a burglar about to do a job, before I went in—I was pretty comfortable there.

They called him "Mr. Smellingscheck", and treated him with a peculiar kind of deference, the reason for which they themselves were doubtless unable to explain or even understand. The haggard woman who made the beds called him "Mr. Smell-'is-check". Poor fellow! I didn't think, by the look of him, that he'd smelt his cheque, or anyone else's, or that anyone else had smelt his, for many a long day. He was a fat man, slow and placid. He looked like a typical monopolist who had unaccountably got into a suit of clothes belonging to a Domain unemployed, and hadn't noticed, or had entirely forgotten, the circumstance in his business cares—if such a word as care could be connected with such a calm, self-contained nature. He wore a suit of cheap slops of some kind of shoddy "tweed". The coat was too small and the trousers too short, and they were drawn up to meet the waistcoat—which they did with painful difficulty, now and then showing, by way of protest, two pairs of brass buttons and the ends of the brace-straps; and they seemed to blame the irresponsive waistcoat or the wearer for it all. Yet he never gave way to assist them. A pair of burst elastic-sides were in full evidence, and a rim of cloudy sock, with a hole in it, showed at every step.

But he put on his clothes and wore them like—like a gentleman. He had two white shirts, and they were both dirty. He'd lay them out on the bed, turn them over, regard them thoughtfully, choose that which appeared to his calm understanding to be the cleaner, and put it on, and wear it until it was unmistakably dirtier than the other; then he'd wear the other till it was dirtier than the first. He managed his three collars the same way. His handkerchiefs were washed in the bathroom, and dried, without the slightest disguise, in the bedroom. He never hurried in anything. The way he cleaned his teeth, shaved, and made his toilet almost transformed the place, in my imagination, into a gentleman's dressing-room.

He talked politics and such things in the abstract—always in the abstract—calmly in the abstract. He was an old-fashioned Conservative of the Sir Leicester Deadlock style. When he was moved by an extra shower of aggressive democratic cant—which was seldom—he defended Capital, but only as if it needed no defence, and as if its opponents were merely thoughtless, ignorant children whom he condescended to set right because of their inexperience and for their own good. He stuck calmly to his own order—the order which had dropped him like a foul thing when the bottom dropped out of his boom, whatever that was. He never talked of his misfortunes.

He took his meals at the little greasy table in the dark corner downstairs, just as if he were dining at the Exchange. He had a chop—rather well-done—and a sheet of the 'Herald' for breakfast. He carried two handkerchiefs; he used one for a handkerchief and the other for a table-napkin, and sometimes folded it absently and laid it on the table. He rose slowly, putting his chair back, took down his battered old green hat, and regarded it thoughtfully—as though it had just occurred to him in a calm, casual way that he'd drop into his hatter's, if he had time, on his way down town, and get it blocked, or else send the messenger round with it during business hours. He'd draw his stick out from behind the next chair, plant it, and, if you hadn't quite finished your side of the conversation, stand politely waiting until you were done. Then he'd look for a suitable reply into his hat, put it on, give it a twitch to settle it on his head—as gentlemen do a "chimney-pot"—step out into the gangway, turn his face to the door, and walk slowly out on to the middle of the pavement—looking more placidly well-to-do than ever. The saying is that clothes make a man, but HE made his almost respectable just by wearing them. Then he'd consult his watch—(he stuck to the watch all through, and it seemed a good one—I often wondered why he didn't pawn it); then he'd turn slowly, right turn, and look down the street. Then slowly back, left-about turn, and take a cool survey in that direction, as if calmly undecided whether to take a cab and drive to the Exchange, or (as it was a very fine morning, and he had half an hour to spare) walk there and drop in at his club on the way. He'd conclude to walk. I never saw him go anywhere in particular, but he walked and stood as if he could.

Coming quietly into the room one day, I surprised him sitting at the table with his arms lying on it and his face resting on them. I heard something like a sob. He rose hastily, and gathered up some papers which were on the table; then he turned round, rubbing his forehead and eyes with his forefinger and thumb, and told me that he suffered from—something, I forget the name of it, but it was a well-to-do ailment. His manner seemed a bit jolted and hurried for a minute or so, and then he was himself again. He told me he was leaving for Melbourne next day. He left while I was out, and left an envelope downstairs for me. There was nothing in it except a pound note.

I saw him in Brisbane afterwards, well-dressed, getting out of a cab at the entrance of one of the leading hotels. But his manner was no more self-contained and well-to-do than it had been in the old sixpenny days—because it couldn't be. We had a well-to-do whisky together, and he talked of things in the abstract. He seemed just as if he'd met me in the Australia.

"A Rough Shed"

A hot, breathless, blinding sunrise—the sun having appeared suddenly above the ragged edge of the barren scrub like a great disc of molten steel. No hint of a morning breeze before it, no sign on earth or sky to show that it is morning—save the position of the sun.

A clearing in the scrub—bare as though the surface of the earth were ploughed and harrowed, and dusty as the road. Two oblong huts—one for the shearers and one for the rouseabouts—in about the centre of the clearing (as if even the mongrel scrub had shrunk away from them) built end-to-end, of weatherboards, and roofed with galvanised iron. Little ventilation; no verandah; no attempt to create, artificially, a breath of air through the buildings. Unpainted, sordid—hideous. Outside, heaps of ashes still hot and smoking. Close at hand, "butcher's shop"—a bush and bag breakwind in the dust, under a couple of sheets of iron, with offal, grease and clotted blood blackening the surface of the ground about it. Greasy, stinking sheepskins hanging everywhere with blood-blotched sides out. Grease inches deep in great black patches about the fireplace ends of the huts, where wash-up and "boiling" water is thrown.

Inside, a rough table on supports driven into the black, greasy ground floor, and formed of flooring boards, running on uneven lines the length of the hut from within about 6ft. of the fire-place. Lengths of single six-inch boards or slabs on each side, supported by the projecting ends of short pieces of timber nailed across the legs of the table to serve as seats.

On each side of the hut runs a rough framework, like the partitions in a stable; each compartment battened off to about the size of a manger, and containing four bunks, one above the other, on each side—their ends, of course, to the table. Scarcely breathing space anywhere between. Fireplace, the full width of the hut in one end, where all the cooking and baking for forty or fifty men is done, and where flour, sugar, etc., are kept in open bags. Fire, like a very furnace. Buckets of tea and coffee on roasting beds of coals and ashes on the hearth. Pile of "brownie" on the bare black boards at the end of the table. Unspeakable aroma of forty or fifty men who have little inclination and less opportunity to wash their skins, and who soak some of the grease out of their clothes—in buckets of hot water—on Saturday afternoons or Sundays. And clinging to all, and over all, the smell of the dried, stale yolk of wool—the stink of rams!

"I am a rouseabout of the rouseabouts. I have fallen so far that it is beneath me to try to climb to the proud position of 'ringer' of the shed. I had that ambition once, when I was the softest of green hands; but then I thought I could work out my salvation and go home. I've got used to hell since then. I only get twenty-five shillings a week (less station store charges) and tucker here. I have been seven years west of the Darling and never shore a sheep. Why don't I learn to shear, and so make money? What should I do with more money? Get out of this and go home? I would never go home unless I had enough money to keep me for the rest of my life, and I'll never make that Out Back. Otherwise, what should I do at home? And how should I account for the seven years, if I were to go home? Could I describe shed life to them and explain how I lived. They think shearing only takes a few days of the year—at the beginning of summer. They'd want to know how I lived the rest of the year. Could I explain that I 'jabbed trotters' and was a 'tea-and-sugar burglar' between sheds. They'd think I'd been a tramp and a beggar all the time. Could I explain ANYTHING so that they'd understand? I'd have to be lying all the time and would soon be tripped up and found out. For, whatever else I have been I was never much of a liar. No, I'll never go home.

"I become momentarily conscious about daylight. The flies on the track got me into that habit, I think; they start at day-break—when the mosquitoes give over.

"The cook rings a bullock bell.

"The cook is fire-proof. He is as a fiend from the nethermost sheol and needs to be. No man sees him sleep, for he makes bread—or worse, brownie—at night, and he rings a bullock bell loudly at half-past five in the morning to rouse us from our animal torpors. Others, the sheep-ho's or the engine-drivers at the shed or wool-wash, call him, if he does sleep. They manage it in shifts, somehow, and sleep somewhere, sometime. We haven't time to know. The cook rings the bullock bell and yells the time. It was the same time five minutes ago—or a year ago. No time to decide which. I dash water over my head and face and slap handfuls on my eyelids—gummed over aching eyes—still blighted by the yolk o' wool—grey, greasy-feeling water from a cut-down kerosene tin which I sneaked from the cook and hid under my bunk and had the foresight to refill from the cask last night, under cover of warm, still, suffocating darkness. Or was it the night before last? Anyhow, it will be sneaked from me to-day, and from the crawler who will collar it to-morrow, and 'touched' and 'lifted' and 'collared' and recovered by the cook, and sneaked back again, and cause foul language, and fights, maybe, till we 'cut-out'.

"No; we didn't have sweet dreams of home and mother, gentle poet—nor yet of babbling brooks and sweethearts, and love's young dream. We are too dirty and dog-tired when we tumble down, and have too little time to sleep it off. We don't want to dream those dreams out here—they'd only be nightmares for us, and we'd wake to remember. We MUSTN'T remember here.

"At the edge of the timber a great galvanised-iron shed, nearly all roof, coming down to within 6ft. 6in. of the 'board' over the 'shoots'. Cloud of red dust in the dead timber behind, going up—noon-day dust. Fence covered with skins; carcases being burned; blue smoke going straight up as in noonday. Great glossy (greasy-glossy) black crows 'flopping' around.

"The first syren has gone. We hurry in single files from opposite ends of rouseabouts' and shearers' huts (as the paths happen to run to the shed) gulping hot tea or coffee from a pint-pot in one hand and biting at a junk of brownie in the other.

"Shed of forty hands. Shearers rush the pens and yank out sheep and throw them like demons; grip them with their knees, take up machines, jerk the strings; and with a rattling whirring roar the great machine-shed starts for the day.

"'Go it, you—tigers!' yells a tar-boy. 'Wool away!' 'Tar!' 'Sheep Ho!' We rush through with a whirring roar till breakfast time.

"We seize our tin plate from the pile, knife and fork from the candle-box, and crowd round the camp-oven to jab out lean chops, dry as chips, boiled in fat. Chops or curry-and-rice. There is some growling and cursing. We slip into our places without removing our hats. There's no time to hunt for mislaid hats when the whistle goes. Row of hat brims, level, drawn over eyes, or thrust back—according to characters or temperaments. Thrust back denotes a lucky absence of brains, I fancy. Row of forks going up, or jabbing, or poised, loaded, waiting for last mouthful to be bolted.

"We pick up, sweep, tar, sew wounds, catch sheep that break from the pens, jump down and pick up those that can't rise at the bottom of the shoots, 'bring-my-combs-from-the-grinder-will-yer,' laugh at dirty jokes, and swear—and, in short, are the 'will-yer' slaves, body and soul, of seven, six, five, or four shearers, according to the distance from the rolling tables.

"The shearer on the board at the shed is a demon. He gets so much a hundred; we, 25s. a week. He is not supposed, by the rules of the shed, the Union, and humanity, to take a sheep out of the pen AFTER the bell goes (smoke-ho, meals, or knock-off), but his watch is hanging on the post, and he times himself to get so many sheep out of the pen BEFORE the bell goes, and ONE MORE—the 'bell-sheep'—as it is ringing. We have to take the last fleece to the table and leave our board clean. We go through the day of eight hours in runs of about an hour and 20 minutes between smoke-ho's—from 6 to 6. If the shearers shore 200 instead of 100, they'd get 2 Pounds a day instead of 1 Pound, and we'd have twice as much work to do for our 25s. per week. But the shearers are racing each other for tallies. And it's no use kicking. There is no God here and no Unionism (though we all have tickets). But what am I growling about? I've worked from 6 to 6 with no smoke-ho's for half the wages, and food we wouldn't give the sheep-ho dog. It's the bush growl, born of heat, flies, and dust. I'd growl now if I had a thousand a year. We MUST growl, swear, and some of us drink to d.t.'s, or go mad sober.

"Pants and shirts stiff with grease as though a couple of pounds of soft black putty were spread on with a painter's knife.

"No, gentle bard!—we don't sing at our work. Over the whirr and roar and hum all day long, and with iteration that is childish and irritating to the intelligent greenhand, float unthinkable adjectives and adverbs, addressed to jumbucks, jackaroos, and mates indiscriminately. And worse words for the boss over the board—behind his back.

"I came of a Good Christian Family—perhaps that's why I went to the Devil. When I came out here I'd shrink from the man who used foul language. In a short time I used it with the worst. I couldn't help it.

"That's the way of it. If I went back to a woman's country again I wouldn't swear. I'd forget this as I would a nightmare. That's the way of it. There's something of the larrikin about us. We don't exist individually. Off the board, away from the shed (and each other) we are quiet—even gentle.

"A great-horned ram, in poor condition, but shorn of a heavy fleece, picks himself up at the foot of the 'shoot', and hesitates, as if ashamed to go down to the other end where the ewes are. The most ridiculous object under Heaven.

"A tar-boy of fifteen, of the bush, with a mouth so vile that a street-boy, same age (up with a shearing uncle), kicks him behind—having proved his superiority with his fists before the shed started. Of which unspeakable little fiend the roughest shearer of a rough shed was heard to say, in effect, that if he thought there was the slightest possibility of his becoming the father of such a boy he'd—take drastic measures to prevent the possibility of his becoming a proud parent at all.

"Twice a day the cooks and their familiars carry buckets of oatmeal-water and tea to the shed, two each on a yoke. We cry, 'Where are you coming to, my pretty maids?'

"In ten minutes the surfaces of the buckets are black with flies. We have given over trying to keep them clear. We stir the living cream aside with the bottoms of the pints, and guzzle gallons, and sweat it out again. Occasionally a shearer pauses and throws the perspiration from his forehead in a rain.

"Shearers live in such a greedy rush of excitement that often a strong man will, at a prick of the shears, fall in a death-like faint on the board.

"We hate the Boss-of-the-Board as the shearers' 'slushy' hates the shearers' cook. I don't know why. He's a very fair boss.

"He refused to put on a traveller yesterday, and the traveller knocked him down. He walked into the shed this morning with his hat back and thumbs in waistcoat—a tribute to man's weakness. He threatened to dismiss the traveller's mate, a bigger man, for rough shearing—a tribute to man's strength. The shearer said nothing. We hate the boss because he IS boss, but we respect him because he is a strong man. He is as hard up as any of us, I hear, and has a sick wife and a large, small family in Melbourne. God judge us all!

"There is a gambling-school here, headed by the shearers' cook. After tea they head-'em, and advance cheques are passed from hand to hand, and thrown in the dust until they are black. When it's too dark to see with nose to the ground, they go inside and gamble with cards. Sometimes they start on Saturday afternoon, heading 'em till dark, play cards all night, start again heading 'em Sunday afternoon, play cards all Sunday night, and sleep themselves sane on Monday, or go to work ghastly—like dead men.

"Cry of 'Fight'; we all rush out. But there isn't much fighting. Afraid of murdering each other. I'm beginning to think that most bush crime is due to irritation born of dust, heat, and flies.

"The smothering atmosphere shudders when the sun goes down. We call it the sunset breeze.

"Saturday night or Sunday we're invited into the shearers' hut. There are songs that are not hymns and recitations and speeches that are not prayers.

"Last Sunday night: Slush lamps at long intervals on table. Men playing cards, sewing on patches— (nearly all smoking)—some writing, and the rest reading Deadwood Dick. At one end of the table a Christian Endeavourer endeavouring; at the other a cockney Jew, from the hawker's boat, trying to sell rotten clothes. In response to complaints, direct and not chosen generally for Sunday, the shearers' rep. requests both apostles to shut up or leave.

"He couldn't be expected to take the Christian and leave the Jew, any more than he could take the Jew and leave the Christian. We are just amongst ourselves in our hell.

"Fiddle at the end of rouseabouts' hut. Voice of Jackeroo, from upper bunk with apologetic oaths: 'For God's sake chuck that up; it makes a man think of blanky old things!'

"A lost soul laughs (mine) and dreadful night smothers us."

Payable Gold

Among the crowds who left the Victorian side for New South Wales about the time Gulgong broke out was an old Ballarat digger named Peter McKenzie. He had married and retired from the mining some years previously and had made a home for himself and family at the village of St. Kilda, near Melbourne; but, as was often the case with old diggers, the gold fever never left him, and when the fields of New South Wales began to blaze he mortgaged his little property in order to raise funds for another campaign, leaving sufficient behind him to keep his wife and family in comfort for a year or so.

As he often remarked, his position was now very different from what it had been in the old days when he first arrived from Scotland, in the height of the excitement following on the great discovery. He was a young man then with only himself to look out for, but now that he was getting old and had a family to provide for he had staked too much on this venture to lose. His position did certainly look like a forlorn hope, but he never seemed to think so.

Peter must have been very lonely and low-spirited at times. A young or unmarried man can form new ties, and even make new sweethearts if necessary, but Peter's heart was with his wife and little ones at home, and they were mortgaged, as it were, to Dame Fortune. Peter had to lift this mortgage off.

Nevertheless he was always cheerful, even at the worst of times, and his straight grey beard and scrubby brown hair encircled a smile which appeared to be a fixture. He had to make an effort in order to look grave, such as some men do when they want to force a smile.

It was rumoured that Peter had made a vow never to return home until he could take sufficient wealth to make his all-important family comfortable, or, at least, to raise the mortgage from the property, for the sacrifice of which to his mad gold fever he never forgave himself. But this was one of the few things which Peter kept to himself.

The fact that he had a wife and children at St. Kilda was well known to all the diggers. They had to know it, and if they did not know the age, complexion, history and peculiarities of every child and of the "old woman" it was not Peter's fault.

He would cross over to our place and talk to the mother for hours about his wife and children. And nothing pleased him better than to discover peculiarities in us children wherein we resembled his own. It pleased us also for mercenary reasons. "It's just the same with my old woman," or "It's just the same with my youngsters," Peter would exclaim boisterously, for he looked upon any little similarity between the two families as a remarkable coincidence. He liked us all, and was always very kind to us, often standing between our backs and the rod that spoils the child—that is, I mean, if it isn't used. I was very short-tempered, but this failing was more than condoned by the fact that Peter's "eldest" was given that way also. Mother's second son was very good-natured; so was Peter's third. Her "third" had a great aversion for any duty that threatened to increase his muscles; so had Peter's "second". Our baby was very fat and heavy and was given to sucking her own thumb vigorously, and, according to the latest bulletins from home, it was just the same with Peter's "last".

I think we knew more about Peter's family than we did about our own. Although we had never seen them, we were as familiar with their features as the photographer's art could make us, and always knew their domestic history up to the date of the last mail.

We became interested in the McKenzie family. Instead of getting bored by them as some people were, we were always as much pleased when Peter got a letter from home as he was himself, and if a mail were missed, which seldom happened—we almost shared his disappointment and anxiety. Should one of the youngsters be ill, we would be quite uneasy, on Peter's account, until the arrival of a later bulletin removed his anxiety, and ours.

It must have been the glorious power of a big true heart that gained for Peter the goodwill and sympathy of all who knew him.

Peter's smile had a peculiar fascination for us children. We would stand by his pointing forge when he'd be sharpening picks in the early morning, and watch his face for five minutes at a time, wondering sometimes whether he was always SMILING INSIDE, or whether the smile went on externally irrespective of any variation in Peter's condition of mind.

I think it was the latter case, for often when he had received bad news from home we have heard his voice quaver with anxiety, while the old smile played on his round, brown features just the same.

Little Nelse (one of those queer old-man children who seem to come into the world by mistake, and who seldom stay long) used to say that Peter "cried inside".

Once, on Gulgong, when he attended the funeral of an old Ballarat mate, a stranger who had been watching his face curiously remarked that McKenzie seemed as pleased as though the dead digger had bequeathed him a fortune. But the stranger had soon reason to alter his opinion, for when another old mate began in a tremulous voice to repeat the words "Ashes to ashes, an' dust to dust," two big tears suddenly burst from Peter's eyes, and hurried down to get entrapped in his beard.

Peter's goldmining ventures were not successful. He sank three duffers in succession on Gulgong, and the fourth shaft, after paying expenses, left a little over a hundred to each party, and Peter had to send the bulk of his share home. He lived in a tent (or in a hut when he could get one) after the manner of diggers, and he "did for himself", even to washing his own clothes. He never drank nor "played", and he took little enjoyment of any kind, yet there was not a digger on the field who would dream of calling old Peter McKenzie "a mean man". He lived, as we know from our own observations, in a most frugal manner. He always tried to hide this, and took care to have plenty of good things for us when he invited us to his hut; but children's eyes are sharp. Some said that Peter half-starved himself, but I don't think his family ever knew, unless he told them so afterwards.

Ah, well! the years go over. Peter was now three years from home, and he and Fortune were enemies still. Letters came by the mail, full of little home troubles and prayers for Peter's return, and letters went back by the mail, always hopeful, always cheerful. Peter never gave up. When everything else failed he would work by the day (a sad thing for a digger), and he was even known to do a job of fencing until such time as he could get a few pounds and a small party together to sink another shaft.

Talk about the heroic struggles of early explorers in a hostile country; but for dogged determination and courage in the face of poverty, illness, and distance, commend me to the old-time digger—the truest soldier Hope ever had!

In the fourth year of his struggle Peter met with a terrible disappointment. His party put down a shaft called the Forlorn Hope near Happy Valley, and after a few weeks' fruitless driving his mates jibbed on it. Peter had his own opinion about the ground—an old digger's opinion, and he used every argument in his power to induce his mates to put a few days' more work in the claim. In vain he pointed out that the quality of the wash and the dip of the bottom exactly resembled that of the "Brown Snake", a rich Victorian claim. In vain he argued that in the case of the abovementioned claim, not a colour could be got until the payable gold was actually reached. Home Rule and The Canadian and that cluster of fields were going ahead, and his party were eager to shift. They remained obstinate, and at last, half-convinced against his opinion, Peter left with them to sink the "Iawatha", in Log Paddock, which turned out a rank duffer—not even paying its own expenses.

A party of Italians entered the old claim and, after driving it a few feet further, made their fortune.

We all noticed the change in Peter McKenzie when he came to "Log Paddock", whither we had shifted before him. The old smile still flickered, but he had learned to "look" grave for an hour at a time without much effort. He was never quite the same after the affair of Forlorn Hope, and I often think how he must have "cried" sometimes "inside".

However, he still read us letters from home, and came and smoked in the evening by our kitchen-fire. He showed us some new portraits of his family which he had received by a late mail, but something gave me the impression that the portraits made him uneasy. He had them in his possession for nearly a week before showing them to us, and to the best of our knowledge he never showed them to anybody else. Perhaps they reminded him of the flight of time—perhaps he would have preferred his children to remain just as he left them until he returned.

But stay! there was one portrait that seemed to give Peter infinite pleasure. It was the picture of a chubby infant of about three years or more. It was a fine-looking child taken in a sitting position on a cushion, and arrayed in a very short shirt. On its fat, soft, white face, which was only a few inches above the ten very podgy toes, was a smile something like Peter's. Peter was never tired of looking at and showing the picture of his child—the child he had never seen. Perhaps he cherished a wild dream of making his fortune and returning home before THAT child grew up.

McKenzie and party were sinking a shaft at the upper end of Log Paddock, generally called "The other end". We were at the lower end.

One day Peter came down from "the other end" and told us that his party expected to "bottom" during the following week, and if they got no encouragement from the wash they intended to go prospecting at the "Happy Thought", near Specimen Flat.

The shaft in Log Paddock was christened "Nil Desperandum". Towards the end of the week we heard that the wash in the "Nil" was showing good colours.

Later came the news that "McKenzie and party" had bottomed on payable gold, and the red flag floated over the shaft. Long before the first load of dirt reached the puddling machine on the creek, the news was all round the diggings. The "Nil Desperandum" was a "Golden Hole"!

We will not forget the day when Peter went home. He hurried down in the morning to have an hour or so with us before Cobb and Co. went by. He told us all about his little cottage by the bay at St. Kilda. He had never spoken of it before, probably because of the mortgage. He told us how it faced the bay—how many rooms it had, how much flower garden, and how on a clear day he could see from the window all the ships that came up to the Yarra, and how with a good telescope he could even distinguish the faces of the passengers on the big ocean liners.

And then, when the mother's back was turned, he hustled us children round the corner, and surreptitiously slipped a sovereign into each of our dirty hands, making great pantomimic show for silence, for the mother was very independent.

And when we saw the last of Peter's face setting like a good-humoured sun on the top of Cobb and Co.'s, a great feeling of discontent and loneliness came over all our hearts. Little Nelse, who had been Peter's favourite, went round behind the pig-stye, where none might disturb him, and sat down on the projecting end of a trough to "have a cry", in his usual methodical manner. But old "Alligator Desolation", the dog, had suspicions of what was up, and, hearing the sobs, went round to offer whatever consolation appertained to a damp and dirty nose and a pair of ludicrously doleful yellow eyes.

An Oversight of Steelman's

Steelman and Smith—professional wanderers—were making back for Wellington, down through the wide and rather dreary-looking Hutt Valley. They were broke. They carried their few remaining belongings in two skimpy, amateurish-looking swags. Steelman had fourpence left. They were very tired and very thirsty—at least Steelman was, and he answered for both. It was Smith's policy to feel and think just exactly as Steelman did. Said Steelman:

"The landlord of the next pub. is not a bad sort. I won't go in—he might remember me. You'd best go in. You've been tramping round in the Wairarapa district for the last six months, looking for work. You're going back to Wellington now, to try and get on the new corporation works just being started there— the sewage works. You think you've got a show. You've got some mates in Wellington, and they're looking out for a chance for you. You did get a job last week on a sawmill at Silverstream, and the boss sacked you after three days and wouldn't pay you a penny. That's just his way. I know him—at least a mate of mine does. I've heard of him often enough. His name's Cowman. Don't forget the name, whatever you do. The landlord here hates him like poison; he'll sympathize with you. Tell him you've got a mate with you; he's gone ahead—took a short cut across the paddocks. Tell him you've got only fourpence left, and see if he'll give you a drop in a bottle. Says you: 'Well, boss, the fact is we've only got fourpence, but you might let us have a drop in a bottle'; and very likely he'll stand you a couple of pints in a gin-bottle. You can fling the coppers on the counter, but the chances are he won't take them. He's not a bad sort. Beer's fourpence a pint out here, same's in Wellington. See that gin-bottle lying there by the stump; get it and we'll take it down to the river with us and rinse it out."

They reached the river bank.

"You'd better take my swag—it looks more decent," said Steelman. "No, I'll tell you what we'll do: we'll undo both swags and make them into one—one decent swag, and I'll cut round through the lanes and wait for you on the road ahead of the pub."

He rolled up the swag with much care and deliberation and considerable judgment. He fastened Smith's belt round one end of it, and the handkerchiefs round the other, and made a towel serve as a shoulder-strap.

"I wish we had a canvas bag to put it in," he said, "or a cover of some sort. But never mind. The landlord's an old Australian bushman, now I come to think of it; the swag looks Australian enough, and it might appeal to his feelings, you know—bring up old recollections. But you'd best not say you come from Australia, because he's been there, and he'd soon trip you up. He might have been where you've been, you know, so don't try to do too much. You always do mug-up the business when you try to do more than I tell you. You might tell him your mate came from Australia—but no, he might want you to bring me in. Better stick to Maoriland. I don't believe in too much ornamentation. Plain lies are the best.”

“What's the landlord's name?” asked Smith.

“Never mind that. You don't want to know that. You are not supposed to know him at all. It might look suspicious if you called him by his name, and lead to awkward questions; then you'd be sure to put your foot into it.”

“I could say I read it over the door.”

“Bosh. Travellers don't read the names over the doors, when they go into pubs. You're an entire stranger to him. Call him 'Boss'. Say 'Good-day, Boss,' when you go in, and swing down your swag as if you're used to it. Ease it down like this. Then straighten yourself up, stick your hat back, and wipe your forehead, and try to look as hearty and independent and cheerful as you possibly can. Curse the Government, and say the country's done. It don't matter what Government it is, for he's always against it. I never knew a real Australian that wasn't. Say that you're thinking about trying to get over to Australia, and then listen to him talking about it—and try to look interested, too! Get that damned stone-deaf expression off your face!... He'll run Australia down most likely (I never knew an Other-sider that had settled down over here who didn't). But don't you make any mistake and agree with him, because, although successful Australians over here like to run their own country down, there's very few of them that care to hear anybody else do it.... Don't come away as soon as you get your beer. Stay and listen to him for a while, as if you're interested in his yarning, and give him time to put you on to a job, or offer you one. Give him a chance to ask how you and your mate are off for tobacco or tucker. Like as not he'll sling you half a crown when you come away—that is, if you work it all right. Now try to think of something to say to him, and make yourself a bit interesting—if you possibly can. Tell him about the fight we saw back at the pub. the other day. He might know some of the chaps. This is a sleepy hole, and there ain't much news knocking round.... I wish I could go in myself, but he's sure to remember ME. I'm afraid he got left the last time I stayed there (so did one or two others); and, besides, I came away without saying good-bye to him, and he might feel a bit sore about it. That's the worst of travelling on the old road. Come on now, wake up!”

“Bet I'll get a quart,” said Smith, brightening up, “and some tucker for it to wash down.”

“If you don't,” said Steelman, “I'll stoush you. Never mind the bottle; fling it away. It doesn't look well for a traveller to go into a pub. with an empty bottle in his hand. A real swagman never does. It looks much better to come out with a couple of full ones. That's what you've got to do. Now, come along.”

Steelman turned off into a lane, cut across the paddocks to the road again, and waited for Smith. He hadn't long to wait.

Smith went on towards the public-house, rehearsing his part as he walked—repeating his “lines” to himself, so as to be sure of remembering all that Steelman had told him to say to the landlord, and adding, with what he considered appropriate gestures, some fancy touches of his own, which he determined to throw in in spite of Steelman's advice and warning. “I'll tell him (this)—I'll tell him (that). Well, look here, boss, I'll say you're pretty right and I quite agree with you as far as that's concerned, but,” &c. And so, murmuring and mumbling to himself, Smith reached the hotel. The day was late, and the bar was small, and low, and dark. Smith walked in with all the assurance he could muster, eased down his swag in a corner in what he no doubt considered the true professional style, and, swinging round to the bar, said in a loud voice which he intended to be cheerful, independent, and hearty:

"Good-day, boss!"

But it wasn't a "boss". It was about the hardest-faced old woman that Smith had ever seen. The pub. had changed hands.

"I—I beg your pardon, missus," stammered poor Smith.

It was a knock-down blow for Smith. He couldn't come to time. He and Steelman had had a landlord in their minds all the time, and laid their plans accordingly; the possibility of having a she—and one like this—to deal with never entered into their calculations. Smith had no time to reorganise, even if he had had the brains to do so, without the assistance of his mate's knowledge of human nature.

"I—I beg your pardon, missus," he stammered.

Painful pause. She sized him up.

"Well, what do you want?"

"Well, missus—I—the fact is—will you give me a bottle of beer for fourpence?"

"Wha—what?"

"I mean—. The fact is, we've only got fourpence left, and—I've got a mate outside, and you might let us have a quart or so, in a bottle, for that. I mean—anyway, you might let us have a pint. I'm very sorry to bother you, missus."

But she couldn't do it. No. Certainly not. Decidedly not! All her drinks were sixpence. She had her license to pay, and the rent, and a family to keep. It wouldn't pay out there—it wasn't worth her while. It wouldn't pay the cost of carting the liquor out, &c., &c.

"Well, missus," poor Smith blurted out at last, in sheer desperation, "give me what you can in a bottle for this. I've—I've got a mate outside." And he put the four coppers on the bar.

"Have you got a bottle?"

"No—but—"

"If I give you one, will you bring it back? You can't expect me to give you a bottle as well as a drink."

"Yes, mum; I'll bring it back directly."

She reached out a bottle from under the bar, and very deliberately measured out a little over a pint and poured it into the bottle, which she handed to Smith without a cork.

Smith went his way without rejoicing. It struck him forcibly that he should have saved the money until they reached Petone, or the city, where Steelman would be sure to get a decent drink. But how was he to know? He had chanced it, and lost; Steelman might have done the same. What troubled Smith most was the thought of what Steelman would say; he already heard him, in imagination, saying: "You're a mug, Smith—Smith, you ARE a mug."

But Steelman didn't say much. He was prepared for the worst by seeing Smith come along so soon. He listened to his story with an air of gentle sadness, even as a stern father might listen to the voluntary confession of a wayward child; then he held the bottle up to the fading light of departing day, looked through it (the bottle), and said:

"Well—it ain't worth while dividing it."

Smith's heart shot right down through a hole in the sole of his left boot into the hard road.

"Here, Smith," said Steelman, handing him the bottle, "drink it, old man; you want it. It wasn't altogether your fault; it was an oversight of mine. I didn't bargain for a woman that kind, and, of course, YOU couldn't be expected to think of it. Drink it! Drink it down, Smith. I'll manage to work the oracle before this night is out."

Smith was forced to believe his ears, and, recovering from his surprise, drank.

"I promised to take back the bottle," he said, with the ghost of a smile.

Steelman took the bottle by the neck and broke it on the fence.

"Come on, Smith; I'll carry the swag for a while."

And they tramped on in the gathering starlight.

How Steelman told his Story

It was Steelman's humour, in some of his moods, to take Smith into his confidence, as some old bushmen do their dogs.

"You're nearly as good as an intelligent sheep-dog to talk to, Smith—when a man gets tired of thinking to himself and wants a relief. You're a bit of a mug and a good deal of an idiot, and the chances are that you don't know what I'm driving at half the time—that's the main reason why I don't mind talking to you. You ought to consider yourself honoured; it ain't every man I take into my confidence, even that far."

Smith rubbed his head.

"I'd sooner talk to you—or a stump—any day than to one of those silent, suspicious, self-contained, worldly-wise chaps that listen to everything you say—sense and rubbish alike—as if you were trying to get them to take shares in a mine. I drop the man who listens to me all the time and doesn't seem to get bored. He isn't safe. He isn't to be trusted. He mostly wants to grind his axe against yours, and there's too little profit for me where there are two axes to grind, and no stone—though I'd manage it once, anyhow."

"How'd you do it?" asked Smith.

"There are several ways. Either you join forces, for instance, and find a grindstone—or make one of the other man's axe. But the last way is too slow, and, as I said, takes too much brain-work—besides, it doesn't pay. It might satisfy your vanity or pride, but I've got none. I had once, when I was younger, but it—well, it nearly killed me, so I dropped it.

"You can mostly trust the man who wants to talk more than you do; he'll make a safe mate—or a good grindstone."

Smith scratched the nape of his neck and sat blinking at the fire, with the puzzled expression of a woman pondering over a life-question or the trimming of a hat. Steelman took his chin in his hand and watched Smith thoughtfully.

"I—I say, Steely," exclaimed Smith, suddenly, sitting up and scratching his head and blinking harder than ever—"wha—what am I?"

"How do you mean?"

"Am I the axe or the grindstone?"

"Oh! your brain seems in extra good working order to-night, Smith. Well, you turn the grindstone and I grind." Smith settled. "If you could grind better than I, I'd turn the stone and let YOU grind, I'd never go against the interests of the firm—that's fair enough, isn't it?"

"Ye-es," admitted Smith; "I suppose so."

"So do I. Now, Smith, we've got along all right together for years, off and on, but you never know what might happen. I might stop breathing, for instance—and so might you."

Smith began to look alarmed.

"Poetical justice might overtake one or both of us—such things have happened before, though not often. Or, say, misfortune or death might mistake us for honest, hard-working mugs with big families to keep, and cut us off in the bloom of all our wisdom. You might get into trouble, and, in that case, I'd be bound to leave you there, on principle; or I might get into trouble, and you wouldn't have the brains to get me out—though I know you'd be mug enough to try. I might make a rise and cut you, or you might be misled into showing some spirit, and clear out after I'd stoushed you for it. You might get tired of me calling you a mug, and bossing you and making a tool or convenience of you, you know. You might go in for honest graft (you were always a bit weak-minded) and then I'd have to wash my hands of you (unless you agreed to keep me) for an irreclaimable mug. Or it might suit me to become a respected and worthy fellow townsman, and then, if you came within ten miles of me or hinted that you ever knew me, I'd have you up for vagrancy, or soliciting alms, or attempting to levy blackmail. I'd have to fix you—so I give you fair warning. Or we might get into some desperate fix (and it needn't be very desperate, either) when I'd be obliged to sacrifice you for my own personal safety, comfort, and convenience. Hundreds of things might happen.

"Well, as I said, we've been at large together for some years, and I've found you sober, trustworthy, and honest; so, in case we do part—as we will sooner or later—and you survive, I'll give you some advice from my own experience.

"In the first place: If you ever happen to get born again—and it wouldn't do you much harm—get born with the strength of a bullock and the hide of one as well, and a swelled head, and no brains—at least no more brains than you've got now. I was born with a skin like tissue-paper, and brains; also a heart.

"Get born without relatives, if you can: if you can't help it, clear out on your own just as soon after you're born as you possibly can. I hung on.

"If you have relations, and feel inclined to help them any time when you're flush (and there's no telling what a weak-minded man like you might take it into his head to do)—don't do it. They'll get a down on you if you do. It only causes family troubles and bitterness. There's no dislike like that of a dependant. You'll get neither gratitude nor civility in the end, and be lucky if you escape with a character. (You've got NO character, Smith; I'm only just supposing you have.) There's no hatred too bitter for, and nothing too bad to be said of, the mug who turns. The worst yarns about a man are generally started by his own tribe, and the world believes them at once on that very account. Well, the first thing to do in life is to escape from your friends.

"If you ever go to work—and miracles have happened before—no matter what your wages are, or how you are treated, you can take it for granted that you're sweated; act on that to the best of your ability, or you'll never rise in the world. If you go to see a show on the nod you'll be found a comfortable seat in a good place; but if you pay the chances are the ticket clerk will tell you a lie, and you'll have to hustle for standing room. The man that doesn't ante gets the best of this world; anything he'll stand is good enough for the man that pays. If you try to be too sharp you'll get into gaol sooner or later; if you try to be too honest the chances are that the bailiff will get into your house—if you have one—and make a holy show of you before the neighbours. The honest softy is more often mistaken for a swindler, and accused of being one, than the out-and-out scamp; and the man that tells the truth too much is set down as an irreclaimable liar. But most of the time crow low and roost high, for it's a funny world, and you never know what might happen.

"And if you get married (and there's no accounting for a woman's taste) be as bad as you like, and then moderately good, and your wife will love you. If you're bad all the time she can't stand it for ever, and if you're good all the time she'll naturally treat you with contempt. Never explain what you're going to do, and don't explain afterwards, if you can help it. If you find yourself between two stools, strike hard for your own self, Smith—strike hard, and you'll be respected more than if you fought for all the world. Generosity isn't understood nowadays, and what the people don't understand is either 'mad' or 'cronk'. Failure has no case, and you can't build one for it.... I started out in life very young—and very soft."

"I thought you were going to tell me your story, Steely," remarked Smith.

Steelman smiled sadly.

Henry Archibald Hertzberg Lawson was born on the 17th June 1867 in a town on the Grenfell goldfields of New South Wales, Australia.

His parents, father Niel, a Norwegian born miner and mother Louisa, a noted poet, publisher and feminist were married on 7th July 1866 when he was 32 and she 18. On Henry's birth, the family surname was Anglicised to Lawson. The couple were to have an unhappy marriage despite producing three children.

Lawson attended school at Eurunderee from October 1876 but an ear infection he contracted left him partially deaf. By fourteen he had lost his hearing completely.

Lawson later attended a Catholic school at Mudgee, New South Wales where he developed an interest in poetry and, on his mother's influence, immersed himself in books given that learning in the classroom, with his deafness, was a major hurdle.

In 1883, after working on construction jobs with his father in the Blue Mountains, Lawson joined his mother in Sydney where she was living with his siblings. Here, Lawson worked during the day and studied at night for his matriculation in the hopes of enrolling at university. However, he failed his exams.

His first published poem was 'A Song of the Republic' in The Bulletin on 1st October 1887. This was quickly followed by other published poems with one recognising him as "a youth whose poetic genius here speaks eloquently for itself."

In 1890 he began a relationship with Mary Gilmore but it broke down due to his frequent absences from Sydney.

Lawson received an offer to write for the Brisbane Boomerang in 1891, but financial troubles at the magazine made this a short stint of only a few months. Despite writing for other magazines in Brisbane it was a dead end.

He returned to Sydney and continued to write for the Bulletin which, in 1892, engaged him for an inland trip where he could write articles about the harsh realities of life in drought-stricken New South Wales. He also took some time to work as a roustabout (an unskilled or semi-skilled worker) in the woolshed at Toorale Station. This resulted in his contributions to the Bulletin Debate and became the experience he used for a number of his stories in subsequent years. For Lawson this was an eye-opening period. His grim view of the outback was far removed from the romantic idyll of bravery and beauty inked in the poetry of his contemporary Banjo Paterson.

In 1896, Lawson married Bertha Bredt, Jr., daughter of Bertha Bredt, the prominent socialist. The marriage ended very unhappily in June 1903. They had two children.

Despite this Lawson was finding his way in the literary world. His writing was achieving recognition. His most successful prose collection 'While the Billy Boils', was published in 1896. In it he virtually reinvented Australian realism.

His writing style of short, sharp sentences with honed and sparse descriptions created a personal writing style that defined Australians: dryly laconic, passionately egalitarian and deeply humane. Most of Lawson's work centres on the Australian bush, it's fabled outback, such as in the desolate 'Past Carin', and is considered by many to vividly portray the real Australian life at that time.

Like the majority of Australians, Lawson lived in a city, but had had plenty of experience in outback life, these two outlooks helped shape a very individual talent. Unfortunately, his life was also flawed with other issues.

In Sydney in 1898 he was a prominent member of the Dawn and Dusk Club, a bohemian club of writer friends who met for drinks and conversation.

Sadly, for Lawson despite his growing recognition and fame he became withdrawn and unable to take part in the usual routines of life. His struggles with alcohol and mental health issues continued to drain him. His once prolific literary output began to decline. At times he was destitute mainly due, despite good sales and an enthusiastic audience, to ruinous publishing deals he had entered into.

In 1903 he bought a room at Mrs Isabel Byers' Coffee Palace in North Sydney. This near 20-year friendship between Mrs Byers and Lawson was a bedrock for him. Despite his position as the most celebrated Australian writer of the time, Lawson was deeply depressed and perpetually poor. His ex-wife repeatedly reported him for non-payment of child maintenance, which resulted in numerous jail terms or periods in psychiatric institutions. He was incarcerated at Darlinghurst Gaol for drunkenness, wife desertion, child desertion, and non-payment of child support seven times between 1905 and 1909 and spent a total of 159 days in prison. He wrote about these experiences in the haunting poem 'One Hundred and Three'—his prison number—which was published in 1908.

Mrs Byers was a good poet herself and, although of modest education, had been writing vivid poetry since her teens in a somewhat similar style to Lawson's. Long separated from her husband and elderly, Mrs Byers was, at the time she met Lawson, a woman of independent means looking forward to a comfortable retirement. She regarded Lawson as Australia's greatest living poet, and hoped to sustain him well enough to keep him writing. She acted as his agent in negotiations with publishers, helped to arrange contact with his children, contacted friends and supporters to help him financially, as well as assisting and nursing him through his mental health issues and problems with alcohol. She wrote countless letters on his behalf and pursued any avenue that could provide Lawson with financial support or a publishing deal.

Regardless of all else Lawson was a vocal nationalist and republican and took pride that many of his works were helping to establish the Australian vernacular in fiction.

Henry Archibald Hertzberg Lawson died, of a cerebral hemorrhage, in Mrs Byer's home in Abbotsford, Sydney on 2nd September 1922.

Lawson became the first Australian writer to be granted a state funeral. It was attended by the Prime Minister Billy Hughes and the (later) Premier of New South Wales, Jack Lang (the husband of Lawson's sister-in-law Hilda Bredt), as well as thousands of citizens.

Henry Lawson – A Concise Bibliography

Short Stories in Prose and Verse (1894)
While the Billy Boils (1896)
In the Days When the World was Wide and Other Verses (1896)
Verses, Popular and Humorous (1900)
On the Track (1900)
Over the Sliprails (1900)
On the Track, and, Over the Sliprails (1900)
Popular Verses (1900)
Humorous Verses (1900)
The Country I Come From (1901)
Joe Wilson and His Mates (1901)
Children of the Bush (1902)
When I Was King and Other Verses (1905)
The Elder Son (1905)
When I Was King (1905)
The Romance of the Swag (1907)
Send Round the Hat (1907)
The Skyline Riders and Other Verses (1910)
The Rising of the Court and Other Sketches in Prose and Verse (1910)
For Australia and Other Poems (1913)
Triangles of Life and Other Stories (1913)
My Army, O, My Army! and Other Songs (1915)
Song of the Dardanelles and Other Verses (1916)
Selected Poems of Henry Lawson (1918)